29P

LAST RUN

LAST RUN

Cynthia Harrod-Eagles

This first hardcover edition published in Great Britain 1994 by
SEVERN HOUSE PUBLISHERS LTD of
9–15 High Street, Sutton, Surrey SM1 1DF.
Previously published in 1984 in paperback format only
under the pseudonym of Elizabeth Bennett
This edition complete with new introduction from the author.

British Library Cataloguing in Publication Data
Harrod-Eagles, Cynthia
    Last Run
    I. Title
    823.914 [F]

    ISBN 0-7278-4679-5

Typeset by Hewer Text Composition Services, Edinburgh.
Printed and bound in Great Britain by
Hartnolls Ltd, Bodmin, Cornwall.

For Sheila Rooney
without whom etc . . .

Author's Note

This novel is one of those which first appeared under the pen-name of Elizabeth Bennett. In re-issuing them under my own name, Severn House has asked me to explain how they came to be written.

People sometimes ask me if I always wanted to be a writer, and the truthful answer is that I always *was* a writer – in the sense that I always wrote. Short stories, poems, essays – anything would do, as long as I was putting words together and "telling the tale". When all else failed, or there was no paper (it was still in short supply in my childhood), I carried on a running narrative inside my head about an orphan girl who lived in a cave in the mountains and was befriended by wild animals.

When I reached the grand old age of ten, I began writing my first full-length novel, about an orphan girl who tamed a wild pony. (I had two perfectly good parents of my own, and can't imagine why I kept writing about orphans!) When it was finished I began a sequel, and then another. In all I wrote about nine children's novels over my teenage years, and even sent some off to publishers, but they were always rejected, though very kindly.

I went to university and went off ponies a bit when I discovered boys. The result was my first adult novel, which again I submitted to a publisher and had rejected. I changed universities, wrote another adult novel, submitted it – and to my utter astonishment won the Young Writer's Award for it. I had never really believed I would ever be published, but that had never stopped me writing. Now I held my first published novel, THE WAITING GAME, in my hand, for the first time. It was a wonderful moment.

However, I still had to work for a living, and with a full-time office job, writing had to be squeezed into my evenings and weekends. What happened next was that I was asked by a publisher to write a series of modern romances for them, to order, and in receiving my first commission I felt I had taken an important step in becoming a proper, professional writer. The result was the Emma Woodhouse novels.

Why did I use a pseudonym? Was I ashamed to put my own name on them? Not at all; but in those days publishers believed that if you wrote more than one kind of novel, you had to have a different name for each kind. I was asked to choose a pen-name, and since I happened to be in the middle of my annual re-reading all the Jane Austen novels, I chose Emma Woodhouse after the heroine of *Emma*. When later another, different publisher commissioned me to write some romances about "career-girls", I was obliged to choose another pen-name, and this time, since I was reading *Pride and Prejudice*, I chose the name Elizabeth Bennett.

In course of time the Emma Woodhouse and Elizabeth Bennett books sold out and went out of print, and they have lain dormant ever since. But when, in 1993, I won the Romantic Novelists' Association Novel of the Year Award for my book EMILY, Severn House thought that perhaps my readers might like the chance to see these early works of mine. So here they are, reissued without disguise. I am very glad to see them again in this handsome new edition, proudly flying the banner of my own name this time, and I do hope that you enjoy reading them as much as I enjoyed writing them.

ONE

WHEN THE first dance interval began Clover escorted her last pupil to the barrier and took the opportunity to get off the ice and off her feet. The area around the lesson desk at Queen's Ice Club was always thronged with pros and pupils and people looking for dance partners, so it was not the most restful place to sit down, but Clover turned her back on the crowd defiantly, sat down and hooked her feet over another chair. She knew she ought really to take one of her more promising pupils on to the ice for the easier dances, but she felt too low just then to heed even the prickings of conscience.

Why hadn't she remembered that the rink was always murder during the summer when the kids were off school? It seemed especially so now, for Queensway had become for some unknown reason a centre for visiting Arabs, and they were always fascinated by ice. The women, masked and veiled, would bring in a dozen children each, ranging in age from five to twenty, and the children would don skates and fall about the ice with no regard for their own or anyone else's safety, making it impossible to do any serious skating and virtually impossible to take lessons.

Only now, when the non-skaters were herded off the ice for fifteen minutes while the better skaters danced, was there any semblance of peace or order. Without knowing it, Clover had begun to watch the skimming figures whirling to the recorded strains of 'The Belle of the Ball' played on an electric organ: one couple in particular caught her eye, bending together at the corners like a pair of young saplings in a stiff breeze. The girl, of course, was one of

7

the pros who taught at Queens, but the man – wasn't there something familiar about the man? When he returned to the barrier after three dances, he passed the place where Clover was sitting and glanced at her with interest, and then gave a double-take of recognition.

'Clover! Hey! Why are you sitting out? Come and dance with me – come on, quickly now, the music's starting!'

Clover, bemused, swung her booted feet to the ground and stood up, and on perceiving how much taller she was than he, she remembered him.

'Gordon – what are you doing here?' she said with dawning pleasure, but he only flicked his fingers impatiently and she hurried to the gap in the barrier and stepped on to the ice, holding out her hand to him. He grasped it firmly and then skated off briskly, almost towing her as he picked up speed to get them to the top of the rink and a patch of bare ice as the music started for the ten-step.

Gordon, small, neat and agile as a cat, had been a professional here at Queens some years ago and he and Clover had become dance partners and had very nearly had an affair, only prevented by her meeting Joe. She had stopped going skating, and had learnt not long afterwards that Gordon had gone abroad, presumably following the professional circuit which moved around the world like the polar ice cap during the ice ages.

'You dance just as well as ever,' he said to her when they had got each other's rhythm again and there was leisure to speak.

'Anyone can dance well with you,' Clover said, hiding her pleasure at his compliment. 'I was watching you with Diana. You're the original rubber man – you adapt to everyone's style.'

'It's the secret of the good dancer,' he admitted modestly. 'But what are you doing here?'

'I asked that first,' she laughed.

'I'm just visiting. Thought I'd drop in to keep in practice. But you – you gave it all up, didn't you? Didn't I hear – wasn't there a man?'

8

'There was,' Clover said.

'Ah! Is that why you were sitting there looking so glum, kid?' Clover nodded. 'What did he do to you, this – what was his name?'

'Joe,' Clover said. 'It's a long story.'

'I like long stories. Come, we'll go up to the bar and you can tell me over a gin and tonic – used to be your drink, I believe.'

Clover smiled. 'You remember that?'

'I remember *you*,' he said, whirling her out of the track of dancers and to the barrier in one slick movement. Not unwillingly, Clover hopped off the ice and they walked up the rubber-covered stairs to the bar. Gordon was a good listener with a sympathetic face: soon, sitting by the big window which gave a view over the ice rink, with a large gin and tonic on the table in front of her, Clover was telling him her story.

'As I remember, kid, you and this Joe were together quite a while, weren't you?' Gordon asked her to prime the pump, so to speak.

'Three years,' she said. 'We'd been living together for a year, and we were going to get married this summer, during school holidays – you remember I was a school teacher?'

'Yeah – the little kids, wasn't it?'

'That's right. Well, anyway, Joe has this friend in America – in California actually, called Arlene –'

'Arlene what?'

'How did you guess?'

'Pardon me?' Gordon looked puzzled, and Clover giggled.

'Her name is actually Arlene Watt,' she said. 'She's some bigwig in local government. Joe met her years ago when she was on a course in London, and they have corresponded ever since. Well, just before Christmas she wrote offering Joe a job over there. It was a very good advancement for him, and of course the money was good, so he was very tempted, but we talked it over and for various reasons he decided not to take it in the end. But then at

9

Easter his company told him he was being made redundant.'

Gordon made a sympathetic face. 'Not a nice Easter present.'

'It could have been worse. The redundancy money was good, anyway, and it didn't take him very long to think about Arlene's offer again. So he wrote to her and she wrote back saying that the job was still his if he wanted but he'd have to come over right away. The money came in handy there.'

'So he went over to California – leaving you behind?'

'Well, I had to stay then – teachers have to give a whole term's notice, you see, so I had to stay on to the end of the summer term – July. Joe packed his essentials and went off, the plan being that I should sell the flat and the bits of furniture we'd picked up, at the same time getting rid of everything we weren't going to take. Then, he was going to fly back over in July and help me take the rest of the stuff to California. Meanwhile he'd have found us somewhere to live, and we'd get married when we got over there.'

'Sounds like a reasonable plan,' Gordon said. 'So what went wrong?'

'Right again,' Clover said. 'Watt was exactly what went wrong. I got rid of the flat and moved into lodgings and gave in my notice and whittled down our possessions to two trunks, and then Joe came over in June, a whole month early. I knew there was something wrong as soon as I met him at the airport.'

'He came back?'

'I have to give him that,' she nodded. 'I suppose he could have written what soldiers in the war used to call a "Dear John" letter. He told me that he'd fallen in love with Arlene and was going to marry her and he'd come back for his trunk and to say goodbye.'

'What a bastard,' Gordon whistled softly. Clover shrugged.

'As I said, he could have written.'

'And you were terribly cut up? I suppose you loved him very much.'

10

Clover didn't answer that for a moment. In the end she said, 'One gets over things. But I'd given up everything – I had nothing left, no home, no job, nothing.'

'Couldn't you have got your old job back? Surely if you told them the circumstances?'

'There's a shortage of jobs for teachers at the moment, you know. I should think there must be ten teachers for every job at least. Oh, I suppose if I'd got on to it straight away, before they'd made the appointment – but then, I didn't really want to go back. Couldn't face it. So here I am.'

'Here?'

'Just temporarily, of course. You know what a sports fiend I always was, and they can always squeeze in a few extra pros here in the summer, so I took a job teaching skating just to keep body and soul together while I worked out what to do with my life.'

'Not this, anyway,' Gordon said. 'You can't make a living teaching kids to stay upright on this rink. Gee, Clove, I'm sorry to hear what you've been through. It must have been rotten for you.'

'The biggest difficulty is,' Clover said, side-stepping his sympathy, 'that I don't know how to do anything except teaching, and there are so few teaching jobs available in England. And then again, I really feel like doing something different. A complete change.'

'You could go abroad.'

'I suppose I could. There's nothing to keep me here, certainly. But what could I do?'

'Do what I do – go on the circuit.'

Clover laughed and reached over and patted his hand. 'Thanks, Gordy, but you know perfectly well that I don't skate well enough to do shows and exhibitions, and you yourself said you can't make a living teaching skating.'

'Sure, but that's only one of the strings to my bow,' Gordon said, sitting back and stretching out his legs, balancing the heel of one skate on the toe of the other and contemplating the effect happily. Clover looked down at her own legs and thought how strange it was that in a

11

skating rink one could expose one's legs to the thigh without anyone thinking it at all arousing, whereas if one did it in the street – 'Sport is sport, wherever you go,' Gordon was saying.

'That sounds profound, but what does it mean?' Clover said.

'I teach skating and tennis and swimming in the summer, and in the winter I pick myself a nice, fat, rich resort and teach ski-ing. Then come the spring when the ice melts, I head off for the pools and the tennis courts again. There are always rich people in this world prepared to pay you to teach them a sport, kid, take my word for it. And the more rich and hopeless they are, the more they pay you and the less they expect you to achieve. Some poor old guys will pay you simply to tell them they'll improve one day if they practise enough.'

Clover wasn't taking it in. 'Ski-ing, now,' she said thoughtfully. 'I don't think I'd mind teaching ski-ing. It was always my favourite thing, you know, even more than skating, but of course you can skate any time in London whereas you have to go abroad to ski.'

'Do you ski well?' Gordon asked, then slapped his own hand. 'Silly question, of course you do. You do everything well, don't you?'

'Not everything,' Clover said ruefully. 'I seem to be a flop in the realm of human relationships, but I'm a fair to reasonable skier. I went twice a year, you know, for years. But listen, Gordy, is it possible to get a job just like that? I mean, how does one go about it? Are these jobs available?'

'As a ski-ing instructor? You're joking! They're desperate for them. There are never enough instructors, because they're such a nomadic bunch, they keep moving on from place to place. The resorts are crying out for instructors – particularly women. Very few women, you know, teaching ski-ing. You'd be a dead cert.'

'But how do you go about it?' Clover asked, cheered by his certainty. He was less useful when it came to detail. He shrugged.

12

'Oh, I don't know. You just ask, I guess,' he said vaguely.

'But how do *you* go about it?' she insisted.

'I guess I just kinda turn up,' he said with a comical shrug. 'And there I am.'

'What if they didn't want you?'

'I'd go somewhere else,' he said with lunatic logic. Clover contemplated an inner vision of herself wandering across the ski resorts of Europe with her entire belongings packed in a suitcase and her dwindling savings in her hand, and dismissed it. There had to be another way.

At that interesting moment, however, one of the barmen came across and said, 'They're calling you at the lesson desk, you know. Hadn't you better go down?'

'Gosh, yes,' Clover said, jumping to her feet, suddenly aware that the dancing had long finished and that she should be down on the ice with a pupil. 'I didn't realise – I must dash.'

'Okay, I'm coming too. Say, how about we have dinner together tonight?' Gordon asked her. Clover paused for a moment in her panic flight to regard him rather sadly. She liked Gordon very much, and would have liked to be assured of an evening in which she didn't have to be alone; but she knew the rules. In her teenager years it had been possible to go out with a number of different lads on a casual basis, but nowadays if you went out with a man, you were expected to sleep with him, so you had to be careful what invitations you accepted. She liked Gordon, but she didn't fancy him.

'Thanks, Gordon, but I couldn't. It was nice of you to ask, though.' She said it firmly enough to leave him no loophole for questions which they asked, she had been amazed to discover, every bloody time, as if a refusal was so incredible it had to be explained. 'Thanks for the drink,' she said, and to make assurance doubly sure she turned at that point and bolted, swinging down the stairs by the handrails like a sailor to meet her two impatient and irate pupils and to explain to them that she now had time to give a lesson to only one of them. *Quel jour!*

The more Clover thought about it, the more the idea of taking Gordon's advice appealed to her. It would certainly be a complete change, and if she didn't like it, she could always come home at the end of the season. She had no doubts as to her ability to teach ski-ing but she didn't quite have the courage to trot off to some resort entirely on spec, little though she had to lose. She would have to prepare the way: perhaps if she wrote and asked if there were vacancies?

Her mind naturally turned to the resort in the Austrian Alps where she had first learned to ski when she was seventeen, and to which she had gone for her bi-annual ski-ing holidays for several years after that. In later years she had gone to Switzerland, but hadn't liked it as much. She had a soft spot for the little village of Gries-am-Zeller; and it occurred to her that if the man who had taught her to ski was still at the ski-school, he at least would know that she was good enough to teach. Though the likes of Gordon might be nomadic, there was something very stable and reliable even at the age of twenty-five about George Reynolds – he had been there five consecutive years when she had visited Gries, so there seemed no reason why he should not have stayed another five years.

In the end it was to him that she wrote, explaining her circumstances briefly and asking if there was a vacancy which she might fill this coming season. She posted the letter, crossed her fingers, and waited. The reply was long in coming. September passed, bringing with it the welcome date of the return to school for the children, and once again the rink was tolerable on weekdays; but it also meant she had fewer pupils, and therefore less money. In the last week of September, when she was wondering if she should write again, or if the letter had gone astray, the reply finally arrived.

It was a lovely letter. He said, of course he remembered her, had always thought of her as his best pupil, and had been sorry when she had stopped coming to Gries for her holidays. He went on to say that they could offer her a place as a ski-lehrer starting on the first of November for a salary of 10,000 schillings a month plus accommodation, the contract to run to the end of March. He hoped that she would accept, and if she would write immediately and let him know he could then give her more information about what equipment she would need to bring.

Clover converted the money, and made it between seventy and eighty pounds a week – not a fortune, but more than she was getting teaching skating, and with nothing much to spend it on, if accommodation was thrown in. In London, the major part of your earnings always went on simply keeping a roof over your head. She was pleased that he remembered her, and delighted that he had so promptly been able to offer her a place. If the money had been less, she would still have accepted, and she wrote back at once to tell him so. As to what she would do after March when the snow would be gone, she had no idea, but decided to let that problem hibernate until then.

Without even waiting for George Reynolds' next letter, she began sorting out her gear at once. She had her own ski-boots, of course, but she had always hired skis at the resort, and she decided that unless George strongly recommended otherwise she would buy skis when she got there. As for clothing, she had a special anorak in anti-glis material that she had bought for ski-ing and not worn for other things, so it was still in decent condition. She had lots of woollen tights for skating, and thermal gloves, and a couple of very cheery woollen caps in patriotic stripes of red, white and navy-blue, but she had no ski-ing trousers.

It was quiet at the rink on weekday mornings, so she took a morning off and went up to the big sports shop in Holborn and browsed happily amongst the ranks of deliciously tempting equipment, and ended up by buying two salopettes instead of trousers. Salopettes were like a specialised kind of dungaree, and were more comfortable for ski-ing for long periods because there was no constriction at the waist since they were held up by the bib and straps rather than by a waist-band. She bought one pair in bright red, and one in navy with a red stripe down the leg, and added a pair of leather ski-gloves to her purchases.

George's second letter arrived with more details. Travel was outlined for her. She would be met at Innsbruck if she could arrange to arrive on the first of November by the two o'clock plane because one of the lehrers was going to be in the city that day. Otherwise she would have to make her way by train. Accommodation would be provided, but not meals, but she would be able to get her breakfast and dinner at a reduced rate at the hotel if she wished. He recommended that she waited until she arrived before buying skis as she would probably want several pairs to meet different snow conditions.

Finally, he said he looked forward very much to seeing her. Ditto, ditto, she said to herself as she folded up the letter. She looked around her drab little bedsitter and heard the sound of traffic roaring outside the dusty window, and thought how in a couple of weeks' time all this would seem very strange and far away. Momentarily she panicked – was she not making a mistake, running away from things, perhaps. It was a big step to abandon your native home and go off to live in a foreign land. She would have done it with Joe, of course, and thought little of it – but nothing is ever so serious when there are two of you. Two of you! She caught sight of her reflection in the mirror over the wardrobe and the bleakness of her expression made her laugh.

'Anyone would think you were going to be executed,' she told herself. 'Instead of which, you are standing on the Threshold of Experience. Who knows what might happen? And anyway,' she added, turning away to make herself some coffee, 'when you've got nothing, you've got nothing to lose.'

It was beginning to snow when Clover arrived at Innsbruck and for a moment she looked at the falling flakes with displeasure until she remembered that from now on snow was a 'good thing' and not to be sniffed at. As she came through the barrier she was accosted by a tall willowy woman in huge sunnies wearing a very fetching outfit of

16

pale lilac trousers and anorak with a matching Dylan-cap perched on her mass of red-gold curls.

'I don't have to ask,' she said, seizing Clover's hand and pumping it up and down with the kind of grip that betrayed the muscular sportswoman's body under the dainty mauve gear. 'I just know you're Clover Cassell. George gave me a description and said I couldn't miss you – "a porcelain shepherdess," he said, and ravishingly pretty.'

Clover was too startled to say anything, and at once her hand was relinquished and the other girl whipped off her sunnies to reveal large, myopic grey eyes behind thick blue-mascaraed eyelashes. She stared into Clover's face with a comical expression.

'Oh dear,' she said, 'You are Clover, aren't you? I haven't gone and made an ass of myself *again*, have I? You know I've done this so often I'm thinking of majoring in Classic Boobs. I once had to meet a Russian couple and had two bewildered tourists halfway to my car before I discovered what they were talking was Swedish and they thought they were being taken hostage.'

Clover laughed. 'No, really, it's all right this time – I am Clover. I was just a bit – unprepared.'

'That's a polite way of saying it,' the girl said, shaking Clover's hand again as if the first time didn't count. 'I'm Rose Dieter, and I'm another of the lehrers at the school, for my sins. I'm convinced, you see, that the Earth is some other planet's hell. I can't see how it would be possible to have so much fun otherwise. Come on, we'll go and find your luggage and then hit the trail home. You must be tired and hungry.'

'Not really,' Clover said, and Rose was off again.

'Of course not. I don't know why one always says that – hangover from the days of boats and trains I suppose. I know what I always want most when I arrive anywhere is a bath and a bloody enormous drink. Does that sound like a good idea? I could arrange a drink before we head off, though not a bath of course. But on the other hand, with this snow coming down, perhaps we ought to get back

17

before the roads get too bad.'

'Whatever you think best,' Clover said, bemused. Rose grinned.

'I do talk, don't I? Just tell me to shut up if it gets too much.'

'I wouldn't dream of it,' Clover said.

'I don't know why – everybody else does. Well, let's get going then. We can get a drink when we get home. Listen to me, calling it home! But still, when you've lived the way I've lived you get to use the word rather loosely.'

'How have you lived?'

'Oh, I'll tell you one day when you've a week or two to spare. It's a long sad bad story. We'll be staying in rooms next door to each other, so don't encourage me to tell you my life story or you may never get any sleep. Not that you'll be likely to get much sleep in Gries anyway — it'll be apres-ski night after night as far as I can see.'

'Apres-ski?' Clover said, puzzled by the usage. Rose grinned again – she had a delightful, hoydenish smile and very white teeth that Clover envied.

'Purely local slang. In Gries, we use the word to mean screwing since that's what all the young people seem to be doing when they're not on the slopes. I'm glad you've come, by the way. When George mentioned your letter, I told him if he didn't hire you at once I'd leave. I wasn't going to be the only female instructor in the place. But I think he'd already decided anyway. He's a good bloke, old George. You know him, I understand?'

'He taught me to ski,' Clover said.

'Oh well, then that explains it. He's the senior instructor now, I expect you knew? All the others are glorious young men – terribly bad for me, you know, because I've never had any self-discipline. I've got my good qualities, but restraint isn't one of them. Now at least the temptation will be halved. What a laugh, the only two females being called Rose and Clover. We'll be like a botanists convention. Still, the lads will be able to plead studying the local flora when they're late for work.'

They collected Clover's cases from the baggage return,

and headed out to the car park. Rose's car was the inevitable Volkswagen.

'I don't think I'll bother with chains,' she said heaving the cases into the back. 'I don't think it will have settled much yet, not till we get up into the mountains anyway.'

She stood for a moment tilting her head back to stare up into the sky at the whirling, descending flakes.

'Glorious stuff, isn't it? There are two kinds of people in the world, I always think, those who like snow and those who don't.'

'What's it like at the moment?' Clover asked, climbing into the jump-seat.

'The snow? Pretty good, and we've had quite a few falls in the past couple of days. We've been ski-ing since the second week of October, and I think it will be just perfect by next week. You fit? Right, off we go then, off to the land of trees and heroes. Or perhaps I should say Confiturembourg, Sugar Mountain in the Land of Sweets. You know, Clover, I think I'm going to like you,' she added abruptly with a smile. 'You never interrupt me.'

TWO

IT TOOK about two hours to drive from Innsbruck to Gries, and the last part of the journey was through the little Zeller valley, flat bottomed, steep-sided, but little more than a mile across, with the River Zell winding from side to side all along its ten-mile length. Villages, scarcely distinguishable from each other, were dotted all along the valley, several of them centres for ski-ing, and Gries was just óne such, perhaps a little larger by virtue of being nearest to the best slopes, but not much.

As they drove, Rose told Clover a little more about what to expect. One of the first things Clover wanted to know was what the accommodation was like.

'We're lucky here,' Rose said, 'we have rooms to ourselves. Some places you have to share – in fact, in one resort where I did a season you had to sleep in a dormitory like nuns. We live in a sort of annexe to the hotel, and you have your own room with a wash-basin in it, and there's a bathroom between two.'

'What hotel?' Clover asked.

'*The* hotel,' Rose said succinctly. 'Not that there aren't others, but they're more like pensions or b-and-b's really. This hotel is right in the centre of Gries and everything happens there. It's got everything – swimming pool, sauna, disco, the lot. The annexe is a small building just behind, with some rooms and some apartments. Six of us live there – you and me and four delicious young male lehrers whom I might lend to you when I've finished with them.'

'And where do the others live?'

'In apartments round the village. There's an old house

on the Dorfplatz where quite a few of them live, and an apartment building – a new one – on the Bahnhofstrasse where the seniors live. All very accessible,' she finished, giving Clover an innocent stare.

'And I suppose it's in this hotel that we eat – what's it called?'

'Hotel Maximillian. The name's a joke, of course: the bloke who runs it, Jock, married an Austrian girl during the war and after the war he couldn't make a go of things in Glasgow so he came over here to run a boarding house. Well, you couldn't go wrong, really. He bought a bigger place and then a bigger one, and now he's settled with this massive great barn, and he calls it Maximillian because it makes a million for him every year. Of course, the locals think it's named after their folk hero.'

'Is that pounds or schillings?' Clover asked innocently.

'Knowing Jock,' Rose said, 'I wouldn't be surprised if it was marks or even dollars. He's as sharp as a hat full of razorblades. I wouldn't like to hazard how many things he's got a finger in. Still, he's not a bad bloke, if you can keep your back to the wall when he's around.'

'Bottom pincher?' Clover asked.

'When there's nothing more central available,' Rose said. 'It's best to keep your room locked at night, even if you aren't involved in apres-ski. Unless, of course, you find you fancy old Jock.'

Clover laughed. 'You sound hopeful – why is that?'

'Only because I'm scared of the competition,' Rose said agreeably. 'Actually it's as well you've arrived now rather than later, because you'll be able to have your pick of the lehrers before the sex-crazed customers arrive.'

'Oh come – it isn't really that bad is it?' Clover said. 'I've heard about that sort of thing but it isn't really like that, surely?'

Rose gave her an incredulous look from her rather bulging eyes. 'You must be joking! That's what they come for, ninety per cent of 'em – it is the wish devoutly to be consummated. It's got to the stage where we're thinking of changing the jargon and starting to call ski-ing apres-screw

21

instead of vice versa. And talking of vice –'

'Don't,' Clover said. 'I'm just wondering when you sleep.'

'On the job,' Rose said with an unfathomable look.

It was six o'clock and dark by the time they arrived at the village, and Clover could get no more than an impression of white snow and black buildings to remind her of the place where she had spent such pleasant holidays. The Hotel Maximillian was just off the main square, built on a corner so that some of its windows looked out on the central statue of the national hero from which it did not take its name. It was a wooden building with the overhanging eaves, balconies and what Clover thought of as poker-work decorations that were typical of the area. In fact, it looked very much like one of those model Swiss chalets that turn out to be musical jewel-boxes when you lift the roof.

It was very large, and the annexe was beside rather than behind it, down the narrow side-street called Spitalgasse, and as Rose swung the car into the space between the annexe and the main building and stopped the engine Clover drew a sigh of relief, aware now that she very much wanted both of the palliatives to travel that Rose had mentioned earlier. The annexe was much like the hotel, but smaller and less ornate.

'We're up the top,' Rose told Clover as she hauled the cases out. 'There are apartments on the two lower floors and single rooms on the upper two, and we lehrers are all on the top floor. But don't worry,' she added, peering at Clover's face in the gloom, 'there's a lift.'

'I'm very glad to hear it.'

The room was clean, bare and functional, and had about it the pleasant aromatic smell of wood which Clover remembered. There was a wash-basin set into a pine-topped vanity unit with a large mirror above it; a table with two chairs; an armchair; bookshelves; built-in wardrobe, and a bed which, if it wasn't a double, was at least a single-and-a-half. The central heating was evidently on, and through the double-glazed french windows Clover could

22

see the snow drifting down past her own private poker-work balcony.

'It's nice,' she muttered.

'They're all identical,' Rose said, 'which can make it very difficult if you come home pissed, but they're very comfortable. Mine's next door, look,' and she led Clover to the next door and flung it open. The room was littered from side to side with clothes, books, pictures, ski-ing equipment, magazines and bottles and jars of cosmetics as if the contents of four suitcases had been emptied into it from a great height.

'I thought you said the rooms were identical,' Clover said. 'I certainly shouldn't mistake this one for mine.'

'Rude!' Rose said admiringly. 'Actually, it's very effective camouflage. Once I'm in there under that lot, even Jock can't find me and the bloodhounds get claustrophobia and back out. The bathroom's here, next to me, and I've arranged with the lads that you and I shall share this. It's nicer that way.' She opened the door of the bathroom to reveal, apparently, the drying-room of a Chinese laundry.

'I see you've settled in here, too,' Clover said.

'I think I might take back what I said about getting on with you,' Rose laughed. 'Actually I think most of this is dry. I'll clear it out, and then you can have a bath or whatever turns you on before we go and eat. We eat at around seven generally, down in the restaurant of the Hot Max. The grub's pretty average – which if you didn't know is army slang for bloody awful – but we get concessionary rates, so unless someone else is paying it's worth sticking to it. Of course, sticking to it is sometimes the problem. Some of the junk Jock serves up seems happier coming up than going down. Still – don't want to upset you at this early stage. Steer clear of his meat balls, though, is my advice. There's only one thing Jock does well with balls and it's nothing to do with *haute cuisine*.'

'Thanks,' Clover said. 'I would like a bath, actually. What's the right thing to wear afterwards?'

'Oh, we don't dress up much. Trousers and a sweater, I

suppose. Shall I come and pick you up at seven? Show you the way to the trough?'

'Oh, yes please,' Clover said, surprised at the diffidence with which Rose made the last suggestion. 'I hope you weren't intending to desert me.'

Rose beamed. 'I didn't want to, but I thought I ought to give you the chance to get shot of me if you wanted to be on your own. Some people find me a bit overpowering, it seems.'

'I can't imagine why,' Clover said.

'What do you drink, by the way?' Rose said, grabbing armfuls of clothes from the makeshift lines and backing to the door.

'Practically anything,' Clover said. 'Gin and tonic, I suppose, mostly. Why?'

'Just interested,' Rose said, and left her.

She discovered why a little later when she was basking in the scented steam of a hot bath, for there was a tap on the door and Rose's voice, 'Can I come in a minute?'

Clover reached out and unlocked the door, and Rose inched in bearing an outsize tumbler which instantly fogged with condensation.

'I thought you might not be able to last out until dinner,' Rose said, evidently pleased with herself, 'so I dashed over and brought you this.'

'Oh, Rose, thank you. How thoughtful of you.'

'Oh, s'nothing,' Rose said, and put the glass down on the shelf beside the bath and backed out again. Clover took up the tumbler and sipped, and then lowered herself happily back down into the hot water. Life was already taking a turn for the better, she decided. It had been the right decision, coming here.

At seven, the two girls made their way down, across the narrow alley, and in by a back door to the Hotel Maximillian, Rose leading the way to the restaurant. While in the annexe Clover had heard one or two sounds of other people moving about, but so far she had encountered

24

nobody. This was soon to change, for the restaurant was already quite crowded, and in an alcove to one side of the room was a long table where, Rose explained to her, the lehrers ate.

'Those of us who eat here. Ten altogether, counting you. Six of us from the annexe, and four who live across the road in the Brau Pension.'

There were four young men sitting at the table as the two girls approached, and they all stood up politely and looked at Clover with interest. As for Clover, she at once realised what had happened to Rose's self-restraint, assuming she had ever had any. They were all quite delectable, with compact, muscular bodies, shining hair, and suntanned faces in which white teeth flashed in politely welcoming smiles. Apart from that, they each seemed to be endowed with more than any man's share of attractiveness. Was there some kind of physical examination they had to pass, she wondered, before they were given a job? Some Richter Scale of heartbreak they had to measure up to? No wonder ski-ing holidays had become so popular in recent years.

'Hello, boys,' Rose was greeting them cheerfully. 'I've brought you a new little playmate. This is Clover, just arrived from England, our new lehrer. Clover, these are the four lads who share our confinement in cell-block A -- Wolfgang, Ernst, Bruno and Heinrich, known of course as Heinz. Or,' she added in a whisper to Clover, 'as he is known to many, Mr Sixty-Nine.'

'Don't you mean fifty-seven?' Clover asked, puzzled.

'I know what I mean,' Rose replied. The four young men shook hands gravely with Clover, and Ernst darted round the table to pull out a chair for her. He was a little taller than the others, superbly built, with broad shoulders that she could almost see rippling under his blue cashmere sweater, and hard muscular thighs that were in no way disguised by his elegantly cut trousers. He had the classically handsome features of a Greek statue, beautifully tanned, thick, straight blond hair, neatly cut, wicked blue eyes, and a drooping blond moustache over a subtle, curling mouth.

'We are delighted that you have come to join us,' Ernst said, or rather purred, in perfect English as he pushed in Clover's chair for her, and at once took the seat next to her even before Rose had sat down. The latter sighed pointedly and said to Clover, 'You see how it is? The rising as against the setting sun. Would you believe three weeks ago they were all over me?'

'Never mind, Rosie, I still love you,' said Bruno, shifting his chair a fraction nearer her. He was also blond and blue-eyed, but burly, older than the others, perhaps in his late thirties, with a broad, cheerful, snub-nosed face. 'I not desert you.'

'Bruno's a Swede,' Rose explained to Clover, patting Bruno's hand. 'Don't let this faithful hound act fool you. His forefathers were the ones who came over to England raping and pillaging. Nowadays of course when he puts the order in it's double rape and easy on the pillage, but the effect is much the same. Now what else can I tell you about them?'

'If you're going to tell me things like that, I think you'd better wait until we're alone. You're embarrassing them.'

'Them!' Rose scoffed. 'Lounge lizards to a man, they are!'

'Oh, well,' Clover said, watching them watching Rose, 'in that case, perhaps you'd better just tell me which one is yours.'

'What do you mean, which *one*,' Rose said, pretending to be offended.

'You see,' Bruno said with a heavy sigh, 'you see what we have to put up with?'

'Clover,' Rose said, pretending great seriousness, 'when you're in a situation like ours, you have to think what's best for the community. You mustn't be selfish about things. Now, here we are, two lone girls amongst all these young men who tomorrow may be going off to the Front to lay down their lives for –'

'Oy,' Clover objected, 'you've got the wrong film.'

'So I have,' she said placidly. 'Never mind, here comes

26

mine now. These four are the ones from the Brau, Kris, Mark, Kevin and Gerhard,' as four young men came in through the street door and made their way over to the alcove. 'That's mine in the front – I'm a true East Ender – never mind the quality, feel the width.'

Introductions were made and the newcomers sat down. Kris, whom Rose had pointed out, was a giant of a man, very tall, very big, in fact looking too big to be a ski-er, most of whom tended to be compactly built. In looks he was typically Swedish-blond, but he spoke with an American accent, as did Mark and Kevin. Gerhard did not speak at all, except in German to Wolf and Heinz.

The food was served to them by two waitresses dressed in black skirts and stomachers and white Tyroler blouses; their hair was plaited in to a crown round their heads. They served the lehrers' table with an air of suppressed impatience, and Clover guessed that they resented the duty which kept them from the tables of the generously tipping public. The food, as Rose had said, was average: an amorphous soup to begin with, then an indifferent veal cutlet with overdone vegetables, followed by ice-cream, plain vanilla. The men drank water or ordered beer, but Kris and Rose asked for their own bottle of wine which was brought to them from a cupboard by the serving-table. It was a giant two-litre bottle, already opened and marked with a number on a label.

'Have a glass with us,' Rose offered Clover. 'You can order your own bottle, you know, and what you don't drink they'll put aside for you the next day. These big bottles are the best value, of course, but it's pretty ropey stuff. All right if you've got a stomach like bull's hide which I believe is what they brew this out of. Want some?'

'No thanks,' Clover said, and Kris laughed.

'I don't see how you could after that,' he said.

'Oh, crikey!' Rose said in a Bunteresque squeak. 'Here comes the archbeako. Cavey!' Clover turned her head to look, and saw George Reynolds coming across the restaurant towards them, his eyes on her.

'Hello,' he said. 'I just thought I'd come and see how

27

you were, and how our new arrival is settling in.'

'Can't you leave us alone for a second?' Rose said indignantly. 'Can't we even eat in peace, without you coming sneaking in trying to catch us out doing something we shouldn't? We don't come barging into the senior common room disturbing you at your vices.' She sounded so genuinely outraged that Clover glanced at her in surprise, upon which her face and voice changed instantly to friendly greeting. 'Can I introduce you to our new young lady, Miss Clover Cassell. Clover, meet The Godfather, Senior Lehrer George Reynolds."

'One day, Rosie, you'll go too far,' George said indulgently. He was evidently used to Rose's jokes.

'Well, you're such an old stick-in-the-mud I feel I have to shake you up a bit from time to time. You think just because you're older than the rest – but Bruno here is older than you, and he still looks down girls' blouses.'

But George's attention had passed to Clover now, and he was smiling at her with such a warm expression of welcome that she found herself on her feet and offering her hand before she realised it.

'Clover and I had met, thank you, Rose,' he said, taking the hand that was offered and holding it rather than shaking it. 'It's nice to see you again. You haven't changed a bit.'

'I'm not sure that's a compliment,' Clover said, smiling. 'I've seen my holiday snaps of ten years ago.'

'I would have said you've grown more beautiful,' George said, 'but I didn't want to expose you to Rose's wit.'

'Oh, don't mind me,' Rose said, turning her back and pretending to concentrate on her ice-cream. 'I'm just part of the furniture.'

'I'm very pleased to see you,' George went on, ignoring Rose. 'Have you finished your meal? Would you let me buy you a drink to go with your coffee, then we can have a little private talk in the lounge.'

'Yes, thank you,' Clover said, stepping round her chair and freeing her hand to reach for her handbag. As she stooped, Rose turned her head and gave her an enormous wink, to which Clover replied by sticking out her tongue. 'We'll wait for you in the bar, Clover,' Rose said. 'If you're not back in an hour we'll send in Ernst and a couple of Alsatians.'

'Thanks,' Clover said. Feeling, no doubt as Rose meant her to, just a little conspicuous, she followed George across the restaurant towards the lounge door. He opened it for her, ushered her to a corner seat with a small table, and asked her what she'd like to drink. She asked for a Benedictine with her coffee, and he went up to the bar to order them.

Clover studied him as he walked across the room, remembering when she had first met him. He would then have been in his early twenties, certainly no more than twenty-five, and she was simply another pupil, another holidaymaker come to learn to ski in two weeks in the Austrian mountains.

She had learnt quickly, but it was in the second year, when she returned and joined his class again, that she had begun to attract his notice. He had told her she was his best pupil, and had given her some extra tuition after the general class. The third year they had greeted each other as friends, and during the lunch breaks in the ski-lodge, up in the mountains, they had eaten and drunk together and had talked. He had told her about himself, and even she, inexperienced and self-regarding as she was then, had perceived the bitterness, imperfectly concealed, in his voice when he had explained how he had been in training for the Olympics when he had had an accident.

'It was simply bad luck,' he had said, though from the tone of his voice one might have supposed it was something more malicious than that. 'A novice skier crossed me as I was coming down the black run. I braked hard, but he panicked and fell, and I couldn't miss him. I went over, rolled down fifty feet of slope, and hit a tree.'

The accident had injured his back, and he had been in hospital for some months. The novice, who should not have been on the black run at all, was unhurt. When

George was recovered, he took up ski-ing again, but his back was no longer sound, and Olympic-class ski-ing demanded nothing less than perfection. Ski-ing was his life, and he could not give it up, so he took a permanent job as a lehrer – he was sound enough for that – and tried to forget his former ambitions.

As he came back towards her she studied him covertly. He was of a good ski-ing shape, compactly built, not tall, but supple and well-muscled. He had a tan, of course, but it was a lighter tan than most, pale gold rather than brown; his hair was dark, looked black from a distance, but when he came nearer you could see that it was in fact a very dark brown, with the reddish sheen on it of a fox's pelt, and it was cut very short and neat. He had the fine skin that went with auburn hair and blue eyes, and it was the eyes one noticed most, for they were very, very blue, dark blue like a Siamese cat's, and fringed with thick, black lashes making the contrast startling.

In repose, his face was sad, she thought as he came towards her, and not really handsome in the conventional way; but when he looked up and saw her looking at him, he suddenly smiled, and a deep warmth spread through her. His face seemed suddenly familiar and dear to her. Beside the ready, trivial glamour of the young lehrers, his attractiveness was breathtakingly real and solid, making the others seem for a moment no more than glossy paper cut-outs.

'Sorry to keep you waiting,' he said.

'It's all right,' she answered, making room for him. 'I was just trying to remember what you were like when I first met you, so that I could tell if you've changed.'

'And what conclusion did you come to?' he asked, placing cups and glasses with care on the table, as if the job were taking all his attention. The moment seemed all at once too significant, and she spoke lightly to hide her embarrassment.

'None! I really couldn't remember accurately at all.'

'I see,' he said, and she thought perhaps he was disappointed, for the smile faded from his face and he became businesslike. 'Well now, I just wanted to tell you one or two things about the job. Firstly, the lesson week starts on Monday. The new guests arrive on Saturday so in the evening we generally have a welcoming party for them which all the lehrers are obliged to attend. On Sunday there are no classes but we have a meeting on Sunday night which again is compulsory. From Monday to Friday the lessons are from ten to twelve and from two to four, and on Friday afternoon instead of a normal lesson we hold competitions and games for the pupils, and we give out little prizes at the farewell party on Friday night.'

'So many parties, so little time,' Clover murmured.

'Almost all the guests speak either English or German, so for practical purposes we divide up the school into English-speaking and German-speaking. I am the head of the English-speaking school, to which you will belong. Now, I don't know how well you remember the place –'

'Pretty well,' Clover said, taking it for a question, and discovering immediately that it was not.

'– but I think it would be a good idea for you to spend tomorrow looking round and familiarising yourself with the layout of the school and the slopes, and next week you can ski yourself in and join in one or two of the lessons just to get the feel of it.'

'I shan't need a whole week to do that,' Clover objected. 'I'm already fit, and I do know how to teach.'

'We'll see,' he said. 'I shall keep an eye on you anyway, and I'll decide if you're ready to take over a group before the end of the week.'

Clover shrugged, accepting his authority, and wondering how much of it was a disguise and how much came naturally to him. He paused now, and had she been looking at him she might have noticed a change in his expression as he began hesitantly, 'I wonder –'

But at that moment Ernst came in from the restaurant and called her name, and she turned to look. He put his hand on her shoulder and said, 'If you have finished, perhaps you would like to come with us now that we go to the *stuberl*? Have you finished here, Herr Commandant?'

31

Clover smiled her willingness at Ernst and turned to George, to see at once that he did not like being called Herr Commandant, or at least that he was put out by something.

'Yes, I've finished,' he said, and stood up. 'I'll see you tomorrow,' he said abruptly to Clover, and walked away. Clover watched him go, a little puzzled. She stood up, and Ernst slipped his arm round her waist and gave her a friendly hug.

'Do not worry about him,' he said. 'The Commandant disapproves of all young people, on principle. Come, Gnadige Lehrerin, and dance the night away with me.'

Clover went with him to rejoin the group, thinking, *But he is young himself. He can't like being cut out by these thoughtless boys.* The group received her noisily, and she shrugged the thought away and concentrated on enjoying herself.

THREE

CLOVER WOKE up the next morning in an absolute panic, not knowing where she was or what had happened. She opened her eyes, stared at the wooden ceiling in the strange snowy light, and gradually her memory seeped back – of course, the welcome party for the new guests followed by dancing in the disco, drinking and general merrymaking. She had left early, unable to keep her eyes open any longer and worn out by Ernst's wild dancing, but she had left them still at it, and not for the last time she wondered how they managed to keep it up and still do a full day's work.

Her mouth felt like the bottom of a parrot's cage, and she very soon became victim to an overwhelming longing for several cups of very hot, very strong black coffee which she had to balance against a reluctance to get up. She could see that she would have to make some arrangements for tea- or coffee-making facilities in her room, but for the moment there was nothing for it but to get up, washed, dressed, and down to the restaurant.

When she returned from the bathroom she saw that the door to Rose's room was open, and as she passed Rose called her to come in. Clover was surprised to find Rose already up and dressed, but a second glance revealed the tell-tale drops of melted snow on her moon-boots and the fact that she was wearing the same clothes as last night.

'Hello! Sleep well?' Rose greeted her. 'I can't imagine why you're up so early. I've just come over to change my top before breakfast – there's something so slummy about wearing the same clothes twice running, don't you think? Or don't you?'

33

'Um – yes. I think,' Clover said, having lost track of what she was answering. 'How on earth do they keep it up?'

'The lads? That's what I always ask myself,' Rose said with a repressed grin. 'Don't ask them, though – they may feel constrained to demonstrate. However it seems to do them good. And I look better for my evening's practice for the Olympics than you do rising from your blameless bed – but then I was born looking shagged out so probably no one would be able to tell the difference.' She glanced at her reflection in the mirror and smiled at it as at a friend. One of the things Clover already liked about Rose was her apparent liking for herself.

'You are looking good,' Clover agreed. 'Are you going down to breakfast? Will you wait for me while I get dressed?'

'Of course. I'll come with you. What are you doing today? Oh, yes, you've had orders to go over the ground, haven't you? Is Ernst taking you?'

'Ernst?' Clover asked vaguely as they walked back to her room. Rose smiled indulgently.

'Yes, Ernst. He's always the first at the counter. I see him as a sort of rough-rider, takes the edge off the new arrivals before the serious work of breaking in starts.'

'I didn't –'

'Of course you didn't, a nice girl like you,' Rose said innocently.

'Rose –!'

'No, I mean it. But he is awfully nice, you know, and I could see he'd taken a shine to you. Mind you, who wouldn't, even laying aside the fact that there are only the two of us? They were all looking at you like Bedouins in Harrods. All I ask is that you lay off my Kris for a week or two until I've got bored with him.'

'I hope you're joking. I didn't come here to –'

'Didn't you?'

'Of course not,' Clover said hotly.

A few minutes later they were crossing the street to the restaurant, and Clover breathed in the excitingly crisp air of the still morning and glanced about her at the glittering snow, the clean sunshine on the pretty wooden buildings, and above the small slice of sky that she could see that was a deep perfect blue.

'It's a lovely day,' she said. Her moon boots crunched on the frozen fringe of snow beside the path that had already been swept clear and then she was following Rose, rather regretfully, into the centrally heated, air-conditioned atmosphere of the hotel. Only Heinz was at the lehrers' table, and as the girls walked across, one of the waiters approached to give Clover a folded note. Clover thanked him and looked at it in surprise.

'Who could be writing to me already?' she asked aloud. Rose grinned.

'Want to bet it isn't male?'

'No takers,' Clover said, opening it and looking at the signature, expecting as far as she expected anything that it would be from Ernst. It was signed G. Reynolds, and it said,

I will meet you at the hotel at ten and take you up to the school to choose skis, and then show you over the slopes. Please be ready.

'That's nice of him,' Clover said.

'What is?' Rose asked, and Clover gave her the note to read. 'I wouldn't bet on it,' she said when she had read it and handed it back. 'Someone official has to be around to give you your passes and skis. I don't expect he likes getting up any more than I do.'

'Why don't you like him?' Clover asked curiously. Rose shrugged indifferently.

'No reason. Just that he's the headmaster, and it's one's duty to hate him. It's them-and-us, isn't it? I don't really *dislike* him. We all take a rise out of him, that's all.'

'Who are you talking about?' Heinz asked as they joined him at the table.

'Guess.'

'The Commandant?'

'Got it in one, Curly. Have a gold star.'

'Please?'

35

'Forget it,' Rose said, reaching over to ruffle Heinz's soft dark hair. 'George has just made a date with Clover to show her the ropes, or rather the slopes, this morning.'

'Oh, that is a pity,' Heinz said, looking at Clover. 'I was going to offer to do that myself. For that reason I have got up early, but it seems not early enough.'

His voice was soft and very gentle, and Clover was affected enough by it to think it a pity too.

'Oh, it's the early worm that gets this bird, all right,' Rose said cheerfully. 'Oy, garcon, ein tasse de café parfavore.' The waiter, who had just arrived with a large tray, gave her a boiled look at her assumed cockney accent, and placed on the table in front of them a basket of hot rolls and a large metal jug from which the silvering was wearing brassily. A wisp of steam rose from its spout and Clover's mouth watered at the glorious smell. Ten seconds later she was sipping gratefully.

'Coffee,' she sighed. 'Saved my life.'

'I know what you mean,' Rose said. 'Here, have a hot roll. You'll have to get a move on if the puppet-master is calling for you at ten.'

'So I will,' Clover said, reaching out for a crisp brown roll and the jam pot. Bread and jam for breakfast would have made her gag at home, but here it seemed perfectly natural. Heinz watched her with the innocent eyes of a baby.

'I am sorry I shall not be able to introduce you to the slopes,' he said in his careful English, 'but perhaps you would let me buy you lunch in the lodge afterwards – at one o'clock, say?'

'That's very kind of you,' Clover said, avoiding Rose's eye. 'Thank you.'

'Good. Then I shall see you later,' he said, and got up briskly, nodded to Rose, and left.

'Say one word, and we're through,' Clover warned Rose firmly before the latter could speak. Rose shrugged and grinned and held out her cup for coffee. A little later Clover left Rose still leisurely breakfasting to go back to her room and get ready for it was almost ten.

The cuckoo clock over the bar was still hiccuping its way through the hour strokes when Clover came back down and saw George standing by the lehrers' table talking to Rose. There was a frown between his brows which cleared and made way for a hesitant smile as he turned to look at Clover.

'Ah, there you are. Very punctual.'

'We aim to please,' Clover replied.

'Did you sleep well?' he asked.

Clover could not decide if he was being sarcastic or not, so she answered with a neutral, 'Yes, thank you. Shall we go, then?'

'Yes, take him away, Clover,' Rose said. 'He's giving me indigestion, watching me like that.' It was said as a joke, and glancing at her Clover saw that she didn't dislike George at all. In fact, to judge by the way she was looking at him she really rather liked him. George didn't notice, however. He was looking at Clover.

'Come on then. I've got the car outside – it's quicker than the bus, and we can do a detour to look at the nursery slopes.'

The car was a green VW with two pairs of skis strapped to a ski-rack on the back. George helped her in very courteously and a moment later they were off. Gries stood at the foot of two mountains, the Rosenberg and the Enzianberg, halfway between the two and framed by a loop of the river Zell, and the valley was so narrow and the sides so steep that almost all of it was in shadow, while the sun on the higher slopes of the mountains was dazzling. The baby slopes were at the foot of the Rosenberg, in a large field by the side of the road, and the incline of the field was so gradual that it was hard to see at first that it sloped at all. A simple rope drag ran from the bottom to the top, and already there was a queue of beginners on their way up.

George stopped the car for a moment and they watched in silence. 'You remember the nursery, of course,' he said at last. 'Generally the first three lessons are held here, sometimes more, depending on progress, of course. Then we take them up on the slopes on Rosenberg. We only take the more advanced pupils over to Enzianberg.' They watched for a moment longer, and then Clover's gaze wandered to the contemplation of the mountains. On their lower slopes were woods of fir trees looking impossibly Christmassy with their dark branches decorated with glittering crystals; above, the great mountains rose massively to their sunlit peak. The sky above was cloudless, and the shadows in the snow unbelievably, vividly blue.

George had followed the direction of her eyes. 'Beautiful, isn't it?' he said softly. She nodded. 'When sometimes I get low, or feel depressed, I only have to look up at them, and then I think their beauty pays for all.'

Clover looked round at him, surprised but pleased that he had spoken of something so personal. He was not looking at her. His eyes were directed upwards, and their blue was deepened by the reflection of the sky. She felt a stirring of warmth towards him for just a moment before he put the car in gear again and said briskly, 'Right, let's go and get the lift. I've got your lift pass in my pocket, by the way. I made it out last night. Don't forget to keep it with you all the time. After a while the operators will begin to recognise you, but at first they will ask to see it.'

He reached one hand into his pocket and produced a pink plastic pass, like an identity card, with a pin on the back and handed it to her. She remembered something a little similar from holidays, except that they had been cards in plastic holders. This was much more permanent-looking, actually printed on the plastic.

'Very posh,' she commented. 'Must cost a bit to make out.'

He smiled without taking his eyes from the road. 'We recycle them,' he said.

It was a long journey up the mountain. First of all they got into a four-man gondola which took them up the first 4000 feet to the station at Achenstein, and there they transferred into a two-man sessellift, an open chair. They were provided with a quilted blanket for this part of the journey, and George tucked it expertly around their knees as, swinging wildly, the chair hurtled them away and over the trees. It was strangely intimate being under a blanket with George, and for a while Clover felt an exhilarating sensation of being on holiday. Below them, the blue snow spread over the mountain, smoothing out its irregularities and concealing its dangers. Here and there a grey outcrop of rock or a steep gulley broke the monotony, while the green of the trees looked almost black by contrast where it showed through the thick white icing of snow.

The initial sensation of speed soon went, and they seemed to drift almost motionless while time stood still. In fact it was about a quarter of an hour's ride, but it was only when they drew near to the station and ski-lodge at the foot of the Karlspitze that they had any fixed point by which to judge their movement. They were getting ready for the dismount when they suddenly broke out into the sunshine, having at last risen above the shadow of the opposite side of the valley.

The ski-school was at the back of the lodge, along with the shop, workrooms and storerooms. The front part of the building was occupied by the restaurant, cafeteria, bar, toilets and washrooms, and round the two sunny sides of the building was, of course, a broad terrace with chairs and tables. It was evidently George country, for everyone greeted him as he passed, at the same time casting interested and speculative glances at his companion as he led the way round to the shop and store, and opened the door of the latter with a key.

Quickly and efficiently George measured her and provided her with a pair of 180cm Median skis and a pair of poles with the new moulded straps.

'I don't suppose you want to buy skis for the moment, until you know what the terrain is like,' he said. She agreed. 'You can hire these for a fairly nominal sum. It will be taken off your wages. We'll go through to the shop and you can sign the necessary form.'

This done, they went outside into the sunshine and sat down on a bench to put on their skis. Straightening up,

George produced a much-folded and crumpled map of the runs, which he went over with her.

'Here we are – here's the lodge and here – that's over there –' he pointed – 'is the blue run. Then there are red runs here and here and here, and black runs here and here. That's up there, but we won't bother with those today. You'll never take pupils on them. If you have black run pupils there are more suitable runs on the Enzianberg.'

'What do you mean, more suitable?' Clover asked. George smiled suddenly, and the effect was much like that moment on the sessellift when they had broken out into the sunshine. She swallowed, suddenly very aware that her fingers as they held the edge of the map were touching his.

'Easier to supervise. It can be tough being responsible for a bunch of adults who think they can ski. I'd sooner cope with thirty complete novices than ten intermediates.'

'It must be a responsibility,' she agreed, gaining an insight at that moment into his frown and his sergeant-major manner.

'It is – particularly when they're paying. You have to make sure they enjoy themselves without damaging either themselves or anyone else, and sometimes the two things seem mutually incompatible. Right, are you ready? Then we'll get the old meat-hook up to the top of the blue and do that first.'

They took the T-bar drag lift up to the top of the easy slope, on which already those beginners who had progressed beyond the baby slopes were making their first morning descents. It was an almost straight, gentle slope, mogulled by the habit of beginners of following the same route all the time. George and Clover limbered up briefly at the top and then made a gentle descent, using it to warm themselves up. George sent Clover down first so that he could ski behind her and watch.

'You have a good style,' he said, when they reached the bottom.

'I should,' she said. 'After all, I had a good teacher.' He smiled at that. 'If you didn't like my style, it wouldn't speak well for you as a lehrer, would it?'

40

'I reserve comment,' he said. 'We'll go and do the reds now.'

The next hour and a half were serious, hard work for Clover, as they ski-ed again and again down the red runs with her in front and George behind shouting criticisms and instructions to her.

'Closer! Get closer to the fall-line. Go with it – don't fight it – keep your movements rounded! Don't bully the curves – use your edges. That's what you've got edges for. Feel the terrain! Good! Good! Now go!'

On the last descent of the morning he changed the process and went in front of her, telling her to criticise him instead, and took her down the fastest of the red runs by the fastest line. Clover quite forgot to shout anything at him, even if she could have found a fault, for they took most of the run at a straight schuss, and she was lost to everything but the exhilaration of speed, the brightness of the air whipping past her cheeks, the dazzling blue glitter of the snow, and the wonderful, unforgettable song of the piste as it hissed under her skis. Ahead of her, the neat, compact red-clad figure of George flew, as supple and graceful and as much at home in its element as a swallow is in the air. She followed him, feeling the delight of her own ability, understanding now with her body as well as her mind what he meant when he had yelled at her 'feel the terrain!'

With two last side-slipping turns they ran out of piste and ski-ed gently across the last stretch of snow to the lodge itself, stopping with a flurry of crystals much as the expert skaters at the rink would fly to the barrier and stop dead, showering the onlookers. George pulled his goggles up over his hat, stabbed his poles into the snow, and turned to her with a delighted grin.

'Well, how was that?'

'Wonderful,' she cried.

'You didn't criticise me,' he said. His eyes were as blue as the sky, speedwell blue against the soft black fringe of his lashes, and his teeth were as white as the snow. Clover grinned ruefully.

'I forgot,' she said. 'I was enjoying it too much. In any case, what was there to criticise?'

'No one has ever finished learning,' he said. 'There's always something you can be told.'

'Tell me, then,' she said, struggling with a glove that had got caught on her sleeve zip. He reached over, pushed her hand away, and untangled the glove and drew it off for her.

'I was going to,' he said. 'You are good. Very stylish. You use your edges well, as I would expect from a skater. I won't say there's nothing I can teach you, but if you teach your pupils to ski as you ski, they'll be all right. You want to get down a little more in the schuss, flex the knees a little more. But you look good, and in my book that says a lot. A person who looks happy on skis is a fair bet to be doing it right.'

Clover became aware that he was holding her hand. His hand was warm and dry and she didn't want him to let go. It was the hand with which he had helped her up when she had fallen, years ago, in her first lessons. Why didn't she remember it? Had it not affected her like this, then? Was it only the unaccustomed strain of ski-ing that was making her knees shaky?

'I was only thinking on that last run that you looked like a swallow,' she said. For a breathless moment his eyes held hers, and then he seemed to become conscious of his hand, self-conscious, perhaps. His cheeks, wind-brightened, grew very slightly pinker, and he dropped her hand and reached down to unfasten his skis.

'Let's go and have a drink,' he said. Very slightly amused, Clover reached down for her own bindings, thinking, he's not as blasé, as self-confident as he appears, for all the authoritarian act.

They removed their skis and stuck them upright in the snow along with their poles, and hung their gloves over the ends, then, they began to make their way towards the bar. All around the lodge the snow was similarly decorated, groups of skis and poles hung with gloves and goggles like fantastic totems, while the brightly coloured figures all headed the same way, for the sunny terraces. Everywhere anoraks were coming off, for the sun was really warm now at midday. Clover took off her woolly hat and shook her hair free, enjoying the feeling of the bright, warm air blowing through it.

'What will you have?' George asked her as they went up the steps on to the terrace.

'Oh, lager please,' she said. 'I'll get us a table, shall I?'

When he came back with the drinks, she had secured a table at the edge of the terrace that looked down into the gorge between the two mountains. Below the terrace rails there was a steep drop of a couple of thousand feet to the wrinkled surface of the glacier below, but it was not only that which was exhilarating.

'Whenever I come back, I always discover I've forgotten just what this air tastes like,' she said, smiling up at him. 'It's so heady, it's like champagne. It's somehow more than just air – one doesn't breathe it so much as drink it. I find myself gulping.'

George nodded, putting down the glasses on the table.

'I know what you mean,' he said. 'It's one of the reasons I stay. Every time I get restless and want to move on, I come up here again, and I look at the view again, and take another lungful of the air, and I ask myself what there is to move on for.'

But despite the words, his tone of voice was sad. She glanced covertly at his face, and saw that he was staring unseeingly at the mountain opposite, his eyes empty.

'Will you stay a lehrer for ever?' she asked quietly, hoping not to break his mood.

'No one stays a lehrer for ever,' he said. 'You get too old in the end, though you can go on teaching babies practically until you retire. But it's a dead end. Sometimes I wonder what ever made me choose a life that can only go downhill.' She saw in time that he had not meant it as a joke. 'You can only get worse at what you do, after a while, and where does that lead you?'

'So what will you do?' she asked. He did not answer at once, and then he glanced at her, and she saw him close his

43

mind to her, regretting perhaps that he had said even so much. He looked at his watch.

'What time is it? Quarter to one. Well now, I think we've had a sufficient look at the slopes up here. What I suggest we do is finish this drink and then ski right down to the village – that's about a ten–fifteen minute run – and have lunch there. Then, if you feel you still have some energy left, we can take the lift up the Enzianberg and have a look at the runs there. I don't want you to do too much on your first day, but –'

She had to stop him, though she hated to, for he had grown cheerful again as he spoke.

'Look, I'm terribly sorry,' she said, seeing his face grow instantly wary as she interrupted him, 'but I agreed to have lunch here with Heinz. He is to meet me here at one o'clock, so –'

'Not to worry,' he said brusquely, his face closed again. 'I'd better be going then. I don't want to be in the way.'

He seemed not so much either angry or hurt but resigned and disappointed in her, which was much, much worse, but there wasn't anything she could say, not possibly, because he had no right to object to her lunching with Heinz and she had no right to suppose that he *did* object. She could not even say, don't be silly, of course you won't be in the way. He drained his beer and stood up, avoiding her eyes.

'Perhaps Heinz will ski with you down the mountain. I suggest you have a look at the route, and spend the afternoon if you can getting used to the terrain. But don't get over-tired, and don't go off on your own. Though I'm sure I needn't tell you that. Ah, here comes your young man. I'll be on my way.'

Heinz came towards the table, smiling a greeting. George gave him a curt nod as he passed, and Heinz turned to watch him go with a puzzled look.

'Our beloved leader seems to be upset about something,' he observed as he reached the table. Clover gave a shrug of exasperated sympathy.

'I don't know,' she said. Heinz reached over and lifted

44

her hand to his lips and gave the ghost of a heel-click and bow, forgetting George instantly.

'Greetings, snow-maiden,' he said. 'Shall we go into the restaurant and eat, or would you prefer to have another drink here first?'

'Let's eat,' Clover said abruptly.

FOUR

THE LEHRERS' meeting was held that evening in the lounge of the Hot Max, as Rose called the Hotel Maximillian. Clover was to discover more and more as she went along that very little that happened, happened anywhere but in the hotel. It was a meeting only for the English-speaking group. The German-speaking lehrers met in a back room at the school's office on Bahnhofstrasse.

They gathered there at six, before dinner, and the atmosphere of having just got out of the bath and being about to go somewhere else made Clover think of children saying goodnight before they went to bed. Everyone looked very clean and shiny and Ernst's hair was wet from the shower.

'How many will there be altogether?' Clover asked Rose as the men drifted in and took their seats.

'There are 25 in the school,' Rose said, 'but if you mean how many in our group, let me see –' she counted up. 'The six of us, and the four from Brau, that's ten, and the two seniors is twelve.'

'Two seniors?'

'George and Valentine.'

'So there's only one I haven't met.'

'Yup. There he is now – nice bloke, but very quiet.'

Valentine and George walked in together at that moment and took their places in front of the waiting group. Valentine was a man in his late forties, Clover guessed, stocky and broad-shouldered and grey-haired, and so tanned that his skin looked like the bark of a tree. George looked round the group gathering their attention and gradually the talking died away, to leave silence except for

46

the sounds in the background as the waiters moved about laying up the tables for the evening meal and the barmen bottled up and washed glasses, all indifferent to the meeting in the corner of the lounge.

'Good evening, ladies and gentlemen,' George began. 'Well, this is our first full meeting of the season, and we have our first full booking. We have –' he glanced at his list – 'a hundred and forty guests in the English-speaking group for this week, so the classes will be quite large to start with, although, as you know by now, many of them drop out. You'll start off with around thirteen each.'

Clover did a bit of quick reckoning in her head and was about to ask a question when George's eye came round to her.

'I haven't counted you in for a class to start with, Clover, as I'd like you just to watch a class or two either with Val or with me. I'll speak to you later about that. As the week progresses there will be a certain amount of movement between classes, according to how well pupils get on, and we'll probably make up a class for you then.'

Clover shrugged and then nodded as she saw a trace of a frown touch his brow.

'Anything you say,' she said hastily.

'Now, lessons. As you know lessons are from ten until twelve and from two until four. You pick up your classes from the terrace outside the ski-shop up at the school or from the bus stop if you are teaching on the nursery slopes. You can make other arrangements with your classes later if you wish, but you must be on the slopes ready to teach by ten in the morning and by two in the afternoon. Punctuality is most important. Any lehrer arriving late for class will be fined.'

Clover was surprised at this, and glanced towards Rose, but her expression, and that of each of the others, told Clover that this kind of discipline was the norm, and expected. That grown adults could be threatened with docking of wages surprised her; but then here in the mountains they were cut off from the rest of the world. She supposed any small group would make its own rules.

47

George went on to outline other rules to do with lessons, what to do in case of an accident, how to transfer a pupil who was greatly ahead of or behind the rest of the class, how to deal with complaints and queries. He spoke briefly about the competition afternoon on Friday and the farewell party that would follow it, and told them there would be another meeting on Thursday night to deal with those things in greater detail. Then his face became grave.

'Now I want to talk to you about your general behaviour, particularly you young men. You are representatives of the school, and what you do, the way you behave, reflects on the school, whether you like it or not. So – and I've said this before but I'm going to repeat it – I want you to remember that you're never off duty until you are in your rooms with the door shut.'

Clover glanced around and saw one or two smirks or concealed grins. Rose caught her eye and winked, and then looked very solemnly at George as if she was hanging on his every word. Clover saw that he had expected that.

'I know it's no good telling you not to mess around with the young female guests,' George went on.

'Too bloody right it isn't,' Rose called out, and everyone laughed, and even George smiled a little.

'Besides, as many of you have pointed out to me, most of the young female guests come here for the specific purpose of – what you people call après-ski.' Another, lower laugh. 'And after all, we are in the business of keeping the customers satisfied.'

'Send them to Ernst,' someone called out, and there was more laughter.

'All right. But remember, there are other guests here as well as the young women. There are a large number of Austrian and Dutch families with young children, and they pay their money just the same. So, lay the guests, if that's what they want, and you want, but when you're in public, behave with decency and, if possible, a little dignity.'

Now there was no laughter. Clover was filled with admiration for the way George was handling the talk – it was pure rhetoric; then she realised that he must have been giving the same speech for years, ever since he first became senior lehrer. Of course he would know the cadences by now!

'And that brings me finally to uniform. The school's uniform is red and white. For obvious reasons – it's easier to spot red against the snow than any other colour. Those of you whose ski-clothes are any colour other than red will have to buy red anoraks and hats. You can buy them from the school shop cheaper than elsewhere and there will be a staff discount. The price can be deducted from your wages.'

Clover thanked her stars that the salopettes and anorak she had brought with her were red – it was pure luck that she happened to like the colour.

'Your clothes must always be clean; you must always when you are in public, either during the day or in the evenings, appear in a neat and tidy condition. If you do not, you will be fined. On the slopes, each of you must carry a bum-bag with a rudimentary medical kit which will be provided by the school. I would like you all to be at the school office on Bahnhofstrasse tomorrow morning at nine o'clock when you will be given the medical kits along with your class lists. Are there any questions?'

He galloped through the last few phrases and there was a dead silence when he stopped speaking. He waited only a few seconds and then gathered up his papers, said a curt good night and walked away. Val followed him, and then Mark and Kevin ran after them, apparently remembering questions they wanted to ask. The rest of the group sat still, looking at each other quizzically.

'Well,' Clover said at last to Rose, 'I never expected anything like this. It's like being back at school. You will be fined for this, caned for that, shot at dawn for the other –'

'Oh no, never that,' Rose grinned. 'As he said, the other is what most of the birds come here for.'

'But seriously,' Clover said, 'how calmly you all take it!'

'Oh, it's always like that. They run these places like military camps. All the ski-schools I've been at are the same. I suppose they have to keep discipline.'

49

'On the slopes, yes, of course,' Clover said. 'After all, it's a matter of safety. But –'

'What the Commandant says is right,' Heinz interrupted her. 'He knows it with the brain, but we know it with the heart.' He tapped his chest earnestly. 'The Dutch and Austrian and German guests, they would be shocked to see the lehrers misbehaving even in the evenings after work. Things are different here. It is not like England, Clover.'

Rose nodded, and said in a low voice, 'You look around you, kid. You see they don't mind. They expect to be spoken to like that.'

'But would he really fine you for looking untidy?' Clover asked. Ernst overheard that question, and leaned over to pull Heinz's hair, which he wore rather long.

'Oh yes, truly he would. Heinzie must have his lovely hair cut soon, or he will have no wages at all. And last year – tell her, Heinz –'

'Last year I got oil on my anorak from one of the ski-lifts. I got it out but it left a mark on the sleeve. I had to buy a new one.'

Clover was amazed. Poor George, she thought. He must feel very isolated, having to maintain discipline over these young men.

Rose now got up and said loudly and cheerfully, 'Well, lads, I don't know why you're all sitting about here like this. You should be heading for the *stuberls* and the disco. Don't you realise there are a hundred-odd young women out there, waiting for you? You heard what the Commandant said – you've got to keep them satisfied. Up, boys, and at 'em! Over the top! It is a far far better thing you screw now than you have ever done.'

'Ah, but what about you, Rose Red?' Bruno asked. 'Are there not many young men also out there waiting for you?'

Rose put on a smug look. 'Not a chance, Bruin. We are young ladies. We don't have to throw it all in as part of the deal.'

'Besides,' Kris said, putting an arm round her, 'there are very few single male guests. And she has all her work to keep us happy here, us lehrers.'

'Keep it in the singular, buddy,' Rose said darkly, punching his arm. It made no impression. His arm was like a rock. 'Well, what are you all waiting for? Gird up your loins. As the doctor said to the lady who didn't like injections, why it's only a little prick.'

Everyone was getting up and drifting towards the alcove table for dinner as she spoke, and Clover watched them, and turned to Rose laughing.

'I hope you talk mainly for your own gratification, because I'm sure they don't understand half of what you say.'

'That's why I'm so glad you've come, Clovy. Now I shall be properly appreciated, instead of having to cast my pearls before this swine.' She punched Kris's arm again, and he gave her a hug as they walked, arms round each other, towards the alcove. 'It's a lost bloody cause, I can tell you. If I was good for anything else, I wouldn't be tramping the world teaching idiots how to ski, and wasting my time with these great thicko athletes.'

'The American expression, I believe, is Dumb Jock,' Kris said imperturbably.

'But how did you get into it in the first place, Rose?' Clover asked as they took their places round the table. Out of the corner of her eye she noticed a small scrimmage between Ernst and Heinz which ended with Ernst sitting next to her and Heinz having to take the seat opposite.

'Oh, the usual way,' Rose said. 'It started off with a holiday romance, only with us it went a bit further. German boy called Karl Dieter. He followed me home, we got married, and then we came back out here. He was a ski-instructor, of course. That's how I learned.'

'What went wrong?' Clover asked.

'Need you ask?' Rose said, raising an eyebrow. 'Look around you, kid. I couldn't stand the competition in the end, so I left him. We're divorced now. We meet once in a blue moon, on the circuit or at competitions.'

'I'm sorry,' Clover said. 'I shouldn't have brought it up.'

'It doesn't matter,' Rose shrugged, and then grinned.

51

'I'm getting my own back now, as you can see. And I can't blame the poor creature – like him I can resist anything except temptation.'

After dinner they all adjourned to the *stuberl* in the cellar of the Hot Max. It was pleasantly decorated, with panelled walls and wooden beams, windows set deep in the walls, little booths and tables, and centre-pieces of dried flowers and candles stuck into chunks of wood on each table. The waitresses dressed in Tyrolean style, and each of the lehrers, it appeared, had his own personal *stein* kept behind the bar from which to drink his lager beer. It was still quiet, most of the guests being still at their hotels, either eating or changing for the evening. The lehrers occupied a corner and the talk was mostly of ski-ing, although after a while one or two of them began to discuss the new guests and mark them for talent. Clover listened and didn't join in. It was all new to her, and therefore amusing. She didn't yet belong to this world, and it had a fantastic air about it. The rules were unrelated to anything in real life, the talk was esoteric, the desires and aims and likes and dislikes seemed as random as children's games.

Guests began at last to drift in and occupy other tables, and Clover watched them, seeing that they were mostly young couples, either engaged or simply courting, it appeared, for none of them looked married, or groups of young girls. The older folk, she imagined, would have other haunts. Now, she saw there was great kudos in being a lehrer: the young girls all looked across at their table as if they were film stars, looked at the men with longing and at the two women with envy. It was probable they did not know Rose and Clover were lehrers too, but simply wondered how one could get into that wonderful, privileged position of sitting at the lehrers' table with such ease and acceptance.

She looked round the table at the brown, healthy, care-free faces, and for a moment felt left out, and wondered desperately what she was doing there. Then Rose caught her eye and grinned and winked, and gave a sly jerk of her head towards the nearest group of craning, lip-licking girls, and Clover laughed and remembered that she had come here for fun, for a bit of this unconcerned jollity that she was finding so puzzling.

'You were looking very serious then,' Rose said, leaning across to her. 'What were you thinking about?'

'I was just thinking that I came here to recapture my lost youth,' Clover said.

'Oh, really?' Rose said, feigning interest. 'Well, tell me what he looks like, and I'll keep my eye out for him.'

As the *stuberl* filled up, the lehrers began to drift off, sometimes to pick up a girl in the bar, sometimes out to meet their dates elsewhere, and so at around nine there was only Rose and Clover, Kris, Heinz and Bruno left. Clover, unable to cope with the large quantities of beer that seemed to be consumed, had switched after the first glass to whisky, and she was feeling very relaxed – perhaps even a little too relaxed, for she had had a more strenuous day than she was used to, and had breathed in a lot more fresh air. She was beginning to feel rather sleepy when Rose said, 'Let's go to the disco. Clover's falling asleep. A bit of healthy exercise will do us all good.'

'I've had exercise all day,' Clover objected, waking herself up. 'That's why I'm the way I am.'

'Ah, come on, you'll never find this youth of yours sitting still. Help her up, Bruno.'

This threat was enough to get her on her feet, and in a moment they were threading their way through the now crowded bar and out into the breathtakingly fresh air. The sky looked dead black above, and the snow was dead white below, without the blue shadows it had in daylight. They pulled their jackets close about them and their breath smoked in the cold air. Bruno sniffed and looked about him with professional interest.

'No snow again tonight. If we do not get snow tomorrow, the cover will begin to break.' His voice rang like a bell in the silence.

'It will snow tomorrow,' Heinz said confidently. 'My scar is aching.'

It was only a few steps from the *stuberl* to the disco –

everything in Gries was arranged around the Dorfplatz. Once inside, Clover wondered a little why they had bothered, for the first people they saw were the other lehrers with the girls they had picked up. The noise was tremendous at first, as was the heat, but after five minutes she had adjusted to both and no longer noticed them. Rose and Bruno went off to the bar to order drinks for them all, and Heinz asked Clover in his gentle, shy voice if she would dance with him.

He was wonderful on the dance floor: his body seemed to dissolve bonelessly into the music. Skiers have to be supple, but their suppleness is more of a compact strength than this fluidity that Heinz displayed, and Clover watched him as she danced with a mixture of amusement and awe. While he danced his eyes never left her face, and she found herself studying him in return. She had barely looked at him before, except to notice he was young and handsome; now she observed his delicate, fine features, the kind of proud, sculpted features that old-fashioned novels always attributed to aristocratic breeding.

His hair was dark and baby-soft, and though he wore it rather long, in soft curls round the nape of his neck, it was well-cut and obviously well-cared-for. Clover couldn't decide if the gold streaks in the front were natural or had been put there, but they were very effective. Under very fine, very arched brows, his eyes were large, and his high cheekbones gave them the effect of being slanted. They were a bright, pale blue, with a very interesting dark-blue line around the iris which made them look wild and rather strange, like a wild animal's.

His neck was long, and his smooth brown throat ended in a tender soft patch revealed by the open collar of his shirt where his pulse beat. He wore a thin gold chain round his neck; what was on the end of it was concealed. His hands, as he held them out to her, she noticed were long and slender with beautifully kept nails, and he wore no jewellery. He took her hands in their firm, gentle grip and drew her towards him. His body was deliciously scented, something elusive and smoky, like bluebell woods. Clover discovered that her mouth was dry and her blood burning, and when he finally put his arms round her and pulled her close she discovered that her body was shaking, with his pure physical attraction.

He felt it too. He craned his head back to look into her face, and he smiled, not a triumphant smile, but a glad one.

'You are not like Rose,' he said finally. 'Rose is too harsh. You are gentle. I like you very much.'

'I like you, too,' she said. He seemed to take it as the answer to a question, for she felt him relax, and felt his hands on her back grow more sure. The beat of the music changed and she was glad to break away from him and dance fast to work the fret out of her blood.

The evening continued as such evenings always do; she danced with Bruno and with Kris and with one or two others. From time to time she sat at the table to rest and consume the drinks that someone was evidently buying her, though she never discovered whom she ought to be thanking; she had shouted conversations with Rose, laughed at jokes and anecdotes, and always, in between other activities, returned to dance with Heinz again. She didn't notice the time passing. She was having fun, having a good time, though afterwards if she had looked back and tried to analyse it she would not have known why it was fun – one never does.

She knew it was getting late by the way the crowd was thinning out and the records being played were slower, but she was still amazed when Rose tapped her on the shoulder as she danced with Heinz and said, 'G'night. Kris and I are going now. Don't forget it's an early start tomorrow – nine o'clock at the school office.'

'What's the time now?' she asked.

'Just after two,' Rose said, and was gone. Clover felt as if cold water had been thrown over her.

Heinz straightened up too, and said. 'What is it?'

'I didn't realise it was so late,' she said.

'Do you want to go to bed?' he asked.

'I think so. We have to be up early.'

55

They left the disco to the last few stalwarts, and walked with their arms about each others' waists the few yards to the annexe door. As they went up in the lift Clover realised that by her words she had probably lost the opportunity to decide what happened next. But she didn't mind. It was so lovely, after so long, to have a strong arm around her waist again, to feel again, however temporarily, that comfortable feeling of belonging. On the top floor they went, sure enough, to Heinz's door, and he fished out his key and opened it without disengaging his arm from her.

The room was just like her own in layout, but it was noticeably cooler than the rest of the building, and it was crowded with pairs of skis, boots, ski-suits, racing suits and poles, while every available surface was covered with framed pictures of Heinz himself ski-ing, racing, posing on skis, posing in groups, or receiving trophies, and with the trophies themselves, cups and shields and small mounted models.

He closed the door and took off his jacket and hung it up neatly. Clover took off her anorak, and shivered.

'It is too cold for you? I always have the central heating turned down very low. I think it is not healthy to live in a room too warm. You feel cold?'

'It's only the contrast,' she said. 'I'll get used to it.'

'We will get into bed, then we will be warm. Would you like some coffee?'

'I'm very thirsty,' she said.

'Best that we drink something, after so much alcohol,' he said seriously. He filled and switched on the electric kettle and then brought her a glass of water from the tap, which she gulped down gratefully. Then she sat on the bed and watched him as he moved about. All his movements were neat and graceful. She saw, too, that though at first glance the room appeared to be untidy, it was only because there was so much in it.

'You seem to have won a lot of competitions,' she said, for something to say.

He looked over his shoulder. 'You think I am vain to have all these pictures around me?'

56

'No,' she said cautiously, because it wasn't strictly true.

'Ski-ing is all of my life,' he said. 'Without the pictures and the prizes, what would I be? I have to have these things about me so that –' he paused and she could see it was because his English was not good enough to explain a concept so far from the material.

'To reaffirm your identity?' she suggested. He thought about that for a long time, and she guessed he was translating it into German. At last he nodded.

'Yes. That's right.' He brought her coffee in a mug. It was real coffee, not instant, and it was black and without sugar. That was actually how she liked it, but she wondered how he had known.

'What do you do in the summer?' she asked.

'I go to Australia and New Zealand. I go where there is snow. Next summer I may perhaps go to America instead, I don't know.'

Clover contemplated with a kind of horror a life that encompassed nothing more than perpetual, continual ski-ing; but after all, if it was what he liked . . . He had finished his coffee now, and waited courteously for her to put down her cup too, before placing his hands on her shoulders and looking searchingly into her face.

'You are very beautiful,' he said at last, 'do you know this? I am sure there are many people to tell you so. Do you have a man, waiting for you back in Englant?'

'No, not now,' she said. 'No man.'

He sighed with what appeared to be relief. 'This is hard to believe,' he said, 'but I am very glad. You are so beautiful.'

'So are you,' she said truthfully, and he paused, startled. Clearly he had not expected that. He smiled suddenly and brilliantly, and drew her into his arms and kissed her. His mouth was soft, sensitive and searching; he was exploring her. She kissed him back, enjoying the smells and taste of him, feeling her desire for his young, slender body rising. She put her arms up round his neck, and clearly taking this for the answer to the question he had never yet put to her, he pressed her gently back on to the bed and eased himself over to lie down at full length beside her, without ever removing his mouth from hers. Clover's body was longing for his, but the part of her mind that was never off duty observed drily to itself that you didn't manage to make a movement like *that* so gracefully without a lot of practice.

FIVE

STILL KISSING her, Heinz slid his hands up inside her jumper and she felt his fingers stretching across her back, searching out the fastening of her bra. After a moment, she put her own hands back to help him, and he pulled his head up and said almost petulantly, 'No, let me!'

She raised an eyebrow in surprise, and he smiled a little sheepishly and enlarged, 'I like to do it. Please.'

With evident pleasure he undressed her, and she let herself go quite limp, enjoying the sensation of his firm, slender hands manipulating her limbs. When she was quite naked, he looked at her for a long time, and she felt his eyes almost tangibly on her skin, making it crawl with excitement. He pressed his mouth to her neck, and then moved it downwards, tracing patterns with the tip of his tongue, running it round each nipple in turn while his fingers stroked lightly down her flanks. She shivered and reached under his clothes, longing for the touch of his skin.

In a minute, he sat up and began hastily to pull off his own clothes, and Clover, smiling to herself, did not imitate his plea, though she watched with impatience as he carefully folded each garment before dropping it to the floor over the side of the bed. He had to stand up to take off his pants, and when he was naked and would have returned to her she held her hand out, palm outwards, and said, 'No – let me look at you a moment.' He stopped, and smiled shyly. 'You are very beautiful,' she said again. The first time she had spoken with insufficient evidence; now she saw how right she had been. His skin was as tender and

59

silky as a newly shelled chestnut, taut over a body that might have stood model for a Greek god. Nowhere was there an ounce of spare flesh, nor any ugly, disproportionate muscle. He had that olive colouring that takes a good, deep tan, so that he was like a bronze statue with that sheen of health on his skin; except in the hollow of his throat, and on the insides of his arms where he was as milky-tender as a child. The fronds of his fine dark hair were like feathers curling in at the back of his strong neck; his eyes looked both wild and shy, like those of an untamed animal.

'Come here, let me touch you,' she whispered, and he moved into the reach of her outstretched fingers. She ran her hand down the hardness of his outer thigh, and was suddenly overcome by his magnificence. She went up onto her knees, put her arms round him, and rested her cheek against his belly.

'I want you,' she said, her voice husky. His pubic hair was surprisingly soft against her neck, and his skin was beautifully scented. She felt his hands touching her shoulders lightly, and when she looked up, she could see his expression had changed, he was looking at her almost uncertainly, and his lower lip was trembling.

'I – I want you, too,' he said hestitantly. She stared for one moment longer, and then reached up and drew him down. He came to her with a sigh of relief, and when his mouth sought hers, they suddenly caught fire from each other, clutching avidly, while pressing belly to belly and limb to limb as if any space left between them were a source of pain. She groaned when he slid into her, and his body arched in reaction and for a moment she thought it was all over. But then she felt his mouth smiling against hers, and knew it was all right.

They made love in a long, slow ballet of limbs and hands, kissing, caressing, moving in perfect rhythm with each other, as sure and as graceful as if they had done it a hundred times before and knew each other's every move. Each moment was an exquisite pleasure that could not be prolonged and yet which lasted for an eternity. Clover had

60

never known such pleasure or such passion. She wanted it never to end, and again and again she heard herself murmur, 'Oh you are so beautiful!' And he would reply, 'So are you, so are you!'

He rolled over onto his back, drawing her with him to lie above him without ever breaking apart, and she leaned up on her elbows and looked down at him, and watched, as he must have been watching her, how each movement rippled across his face, how the pleasure reflected itself almost like pain in his expression.

So many emotions, human beings have, and so few grimaces to express them! When at last they came, he cried out and his face contorted as if with real, unendurable pain; and she supposed hers did the same. Then she collapsed against him, and they lay, limbs intertwined, panting like spent runners. Heinz's hand came up feebly to stroke her hair, and she kissed his cheek and neck gently, feeling great affection for him, and a strange kind of gratitude. Perhaps he felt the same, for he murmured, 'Thank you. That was so lovely.' And then he was asleep.

Clover drifted awhile, and then stirred and woke, discovering she had pins and needles in one hand which was trapped under Heinz's shoulder. She leaned up and gently extricated her fingers, but he did not even stir, so heavily was he sleeping, and when she thought of the long day ski-ing, and then drinking and dancing all evening, and then lovemaking, she was not surprised that he was out for the count. She was only surprised that she was so wakeful.

She looked down into his face, tracing its lines with her eye. His eyelids lay full and smooth and glossy over his eyes, his cheek bloomed against the thick, soft crescent of his eyelashes, his mouth was relaxed, the silken lips lightly together. All the lines of the day were washed away by the deepness of his relaxation, and Clover smiled, feeling suddenly an overwhelming tenderness towards him.

I'll let him sleep quietly, she thought, and began gently to draw away, meaning to go and finish the night in her own bed. But as soon as the air touched his skin where their bodies had been together, he moaned and reached for her, and half-waking, he pulled her down against him, settling her in the crook of his arms, drawing her head onto his shoulder and cradling it with his other hand, stroking her cheek softly and murmuring sleepy endearments. The tenderness gave way before a feeling of peace and security, and without even thinking how strange it was that she could feel both things towards the same person, Clover relaxed into his arms, and slept.

She must have been very tired, for though the bed was small and the night was short, she slept so heavily that she woke the next morning feeling refreshed and not at all dismayed at the thought of an early start. Heinz woke at the same moment, kissed her on the forehead, and then jumped out of bed saying, 'Good morning! We must get up. It is half past seven, and we must be at the office at nine o'clock. I think you have slept well.'

'I think I have, too,' Clover said, sitting up and stretching luxuriously. They looked at each other shyly, and then smiled. It was all right. He looked as beautiful the morning after as he had the night before, and she could see from his expression that she did to him, too. 'I want a bath. What a pity I have to put my clothes on to go to the bathroom.'

Heinz had already pulled on a navy-blue towelling robe which did exciting things for his colouring.

'Do you have a dressing gown?' he asked.

'Yes, but in my room,' she said. He smiled.

'No problem. I will fetch it for you.' While he was out of the room she got up and went over to the window and looked out at the day. It was a fantastic sight, the sky streaked with orange and throwing weird glowing reflections on to the snow. The snow itself looked as downy as an eider duck's breast – there had been a new fall during the night, and it was so billowy and unmarked that Clover felt the old childhood longing to rush out and be the first one to make tracks in its virgin expanse.

62

Heinz came back with her robe, and suddenly she turned to him and stretched her arms out to either side exuberantly and cried, 'There's been snow. Isn't it *beautiful*!'

He laughed, catching her mood, and came over to her, not looking out of the window at all. He dropped the robe and ran his hands up and down her sides, and she arched with the sheer tactile pleasure.

'*You* are,' he said. 'But what a pity we woke up so late. If there was more time now –'

She both saw and felt what he meant, and moved aside hastily, reaching for the dropped robe.

'Ah, but there isn't, I'm afraid,' she said. 'I must have a bath, and I'm absolutely dropping with hunger and thirst. We must wait until this evening.'

'This evening is a long time away,' he said sorrowfully, 'and we must spend some time with the guests also, before we can go away on our own. *Ach so, was wird –*'

'Never mind,' she said consolingly. 'We'll survive.' She put on the robe, kissed him lightly on the lips, and headed cheerfully for her room to pick up her sponge bag.

On her way back from the bathroom she met Rose.

'Don't speak,' Rose said dramatically before Clover could open her mouth. 'I think I'm dissolving slowly in a bath of acid.'

'Good morning,' Clover said sweetly. Rose hauled one eyelid up a fraction and glared at her from under it.

'That,' she said, 'is entirely a matter of opinion.'

'Yup,' Clover said.

'Oh, I see – like that is it? Henry came up to scratch did he? Don't answer that, I can tell by the beastly smug expression on your face. If only he was my type I'd swap you.'

Clover shook her head. 'There's not much wrong with your *brain*, at any rate.'

'It isn't my brain that's been marinaded in liquor and frustration.'

'Oh. Kris not up to scratch?'

'He scratched before he was even under starter's orders.

He's looking utterly poached this morning – eyes like raspberry sorbets. That'll teach him to mix his drinks.'

'You looked all right when you left,' Clover said. 'In fact you left before us.'

'We met two tourists on our way back. Two female tourists.'

'Oh.'

'And got invited up to their room for a party.'

'Oh.'

'The trouble with Kris is he's getting old. He's twenty-seven, you know. At his age, he ought to be more careful.' Rose drew her dignity round her with that parting remark and trudged onwards to the bathroom. Clover grinned sympathetically at her departing back, and scooted back to her room to dress in haste and get down to the restaurant. She wanted breakfast. And coffee. Lots of it. Lots of both.

There was a kind of controlled mayhem at the school office as twenty-five lehrers milled around for their class lists and instructions together with queries and problems in two languages, but the seniors and the administrative staff coped admirably. Clover thought it best to stay out of the way until most of the crowd had dispersed, for if she was not actually taking a class she would only add to the confusion by demanding attention. A number of pupils had arrived early, too, and were wandering about looking for their instructors or for someone to tell them what to do. With a wry smile Clover saw Heinz, looking absurdly, impishly young with his hair tucked up inside his red ski-hat and wearing his goggles fashionably over it, being buttonholed by two young and beautiful American girls who, it seemed, had been in his class last week and wanted to be sure of staying with him this week. He walked away from the office talking volubly, and they took one of his arms each and went with him, exercising their fascination as they went.

Clover had been waiting for George to emerge from the

heart of the fray so that she could ask him what to do, but as he was watching Heinz's annexation Valentine came up to her and said, 'Do you want to come with me? George wants you to watch my lesson this morning, just to get the hang of how we do things round here. I've got a class of beginners on the nursery slope. We can go down in my car, if you like.'

'Fine – whatever you say.'

'And after lunch, I've got intermediates up at Karlspitze, which should be more interesting for you. Do you want to go back to the hotel first and get another jumper? It can be pretty cold standing around watching a beginners' class.'

'Oh, I won't stand around and watch. I'll join in,' Clover smiled. 'I can do everything wrong, and give you an object lesson to work on for the rest.'

'Better do everything right, and give them encouragement,' Val said, walking with her towards his car. 'You'll find as you go along that the greatest problem with teaching adults isn't physical, it's psychological. About seventy per cent, may be more, of them are slope-shy, even on the baby slopes, which, let's face it, are so shallow you've a job telling which way is up. But I suppose it's understandable enough. When you've spent your entire adult life learning to stay upright, it's hard to do anything that might put you in the position of falling over.'

Clover nodded. 'Yes, I've come across that with teaching adults to skate. Kid's are easier – they don't mind falling down, and they haven't so far to fall anyway. But adults are so terrified of falling they go rigid, and they'll flail about in the most ungainly manner, rather than let go and fall gracefully.'

'Exactly,' Val said. 'Well, you'll find the same thing with ski-ing, except that with the worst cases of slope-shyness they won't move at all.'

'And what do you do then?' Clover asked. Val shrugged.

'Leave 'em. There's nothing you can do. They pay good money to learn, but if they won't, you can't force 'em.

Sometimes, if they're left alone they get bored and have a go rather than do nothing. But the chronic cases will drop out after one lesson or maybe two. That's why we can afford to over-book the classes.'

Looked at objectively, the morning was pretty boring, for in the very first lesson of all with beginners, they did hardly any actual ski-ing. Val introduced himself and learned the names of his pupils – it was all Christian names, Clover noticed; that was the American influence – and then taught them how to put on their skis, how to stand in them, and how to hold the poles. All this happened on the edge of the field, and so next he taught them how to walk on skis, in order to get them out into the field proper. The rest of the lesson was taken up with teaching them how to lift up one ski and then the other, and how to turn on the spot by doing a star-turn. To the one or two who picked that up quickly he showed how to do the kick-turn as well.

That was all there was time for in the two-hour lesson, but Clover found plenty to occupy her attention. It was a long time since she had been in a beginner class, and it was salutory for her to rediscover how awkward most people found skis when they first put them on. All around the field there were little groups of people, the lehrer to each class easily distinguishable by his red clothes, and all were learning much the same things. She tried to put herself in the place of one of the beginners, trying to project her mind into their situation, and it was difficult, but very worth while.

She also found it interesting to observe Val and how he handled the class. His age and air of authority and experience, she realised, gave the pupils confidence – they felt they could trust him, and that he would not laugh at their mistakes. She wondered briefly how the younger men managed, and quickly answered herself – they used their sex-appeal, of course. Val gave the impression of being kindly, easy-going, and unflappable. He made little jokes all the time which, though they were not particularly funny, always got a good laugh. Nervous people will laugh at anything, Clover observed, and stored the hint up for future use. He was also quick to be on the spot when anyone fell, particularly when it was a young woman, and he was very solicitous with them, almost flirtatiously so.

Oh, it was a good act, she thought, and very effective. Her own teaching experiences had been different. When she had taught in school, she had of course been teaching children; and when she had taught adults skating, it was always on a one-to-one basis, all her skating lessons being for individuals. Coping with a class of adults was a different matter, and she said so to Val when the lesson was over.

'They were wondering who you were, too,' he told her. 'It was quite funny to see them watching you and wondering whether you ought to be there or not. You being all in red made them naturally think you were a lehrer. That's a big factor in our favour, you know, the uniform. Confers immediate authority. I could see one or two of them about to ask you questions, and then stopping themselves. Oh, you'll be all right, don't worry.'

'Thanks,' Clover said. 'What now?'

He looked at her perhaps slightly speculatively. 'I thought if you'd like it we might go up on the ski-lift to Rosenhof and have lunch at the inn there, and then ski down to the lodge in time for the afternoon class. I'd quite like to see you perform.'

She studied his face carefully, for there was something in that last sentence – and then she saw the hidden laughter. She grinned.

'I'm sure you would,' she said. 'Yes, all right, let's do that. It sounds fun.'

'It could be,' Val said, taking her arm in a way that was half friendly, half seductive. 'If we could manage to get lost on the way down – I know a little hut just off the trail up there. With a bit of luck we might get a white-out and have to spend a couple of days there.'

'Alone – together?' she asked in a tremulous voice. He gave an evil cackle.

'Quite alone, my dear. You aren't afraid of me, are you?'

'You do that astonishingly well,' she said in her normal voice. He continued to leer.

'Practice,' he said. 'What do you think all these notches in my poles are?'

Clover threw up her hands. 'And I thought you were just a clumsy skier!'

Rosenhof was one of the tiny villages up on the mountain which had expanded in recent years with the coming of the skiers. The village inn, which had been no more than a tiny cottage, had been enlarged and then enlarged again to a reasonably sized ski-lodge, and it had a restaurant with a much-advertised view over the gorge between the two mountains. One wall of the restaurant was entirely of glass, and the view was indeed magnificent, well worth coming for, even had the food not also been good. Clover and Val had a window-side table, and they gazed at the deeply shadowed gorge and the frowning north face of the Enzianberg while consuming a very good schnitzel with kohlrabi salad and a bottle of very cold Niersteiner.

'This is lovely,' Clover said with a gesture that included the food, the view and the company.

'So are you,' Val said. 'Much too decorative for this place. What are you doing here, anyway?'

Clover told her story, suitably muted, and Val listened with sympathetic interest.

'Well, I can quite see that you'd want a break, something completely different as they say, for a while. But you won't want to stay for long doing a dead-end job like this.'

'Won't I?'

'No,' Val said firmly. 'You're too intelligent.'

'But you're intelligent,' Clover protested. Val smiled a slightly crooked smile.

'Not really. Only in the sense that a dog is intelligent when it seems to understand what you're saying. And I'm

68

lazy. I like having my life organised for me. If I weren't here I'd probably have joined the army. It's the same sort of thing – house, food and clothes provided, the day mapped out, nothing to do but follow orders. Oh, there's a lot to be said for it, if you're lazy like me. But you – I've an idea you've already had to stop yourself bucking at the orders being given you.'

'You're very observant,' Clover said.

'That's what I meant by my doggy intelligence,' Val said. 'I like people, and I watch them. You won't stay long here. The thing that amazes me, is how long George has stayed here – he doesn't belong to this life either. He *was* ambitious.'

'But he had an accident –' Clover said hesitantly, for she really didn't know him very well. Val looked at her with interest.

'He taught you, didn't he?' Clover nodded. 'I shall be interested in watching you ski, to see if I can tell. He's a very stylish performer. Yes, I know about his accident. That's what surprises me, that knowing he can't ever be a world-class skier he still goes on teaching with a lot of dead-beats.'

'Oh, come,' Clover said, 'you can't call all those stunning young men dead-beats.'

'No, that's true,' Val said, refilling her glass for her. 'The life's all right for the youngsters. They've got it all before them.'

'George doesn't seem to be popular with the youngsters,' Clover said hesitantly.

'That's partly his job,' Val said, 'to be the focus of dislike. It binds them together. But I think they make him uneasy, anyway. I think he's lost his nerve. Oh, not as a skier,' he added as he saw the protest form on her lips, 'but as a person. That's why he gets jealous of the young men.'

Clover had nothing to say to that, and Val waved it away with his hand. 'Enough about George, anyway. I just didn't want you to get the wrong idea about him. His isolation isn't really his choice, it's the job.' He took a sip of his wine to punctuate the conversation. 'Do you want anything more to eat? Or to drink?'

'No, thanks,' Clover said. 'It was lovely, but if we've got to ski, I'd better not have anything else.'

'That's the problem with lunch,' Val said. 'What you and I must do is go somewhere in the evening and dine properly, in a civilised manner, wearing proper clothes. Dinner without ski-boots? How does that sound to you?'

'Charming,' Clover said, not knowing how seriously he meant it.

'Right then. What about Thursday night? Weekends are hopeless, with all the compulsory activities. We'll dress up properly and drive to a restaurant down the valley and have a slap-up evening. Is it a date?'

Clover accepted without hesitation. 'It sounds lovely.' But she wondered for the merest part of a second how much was meant by it, and then she pushed the thought away, angry with herself. He was not like the young lehrers. He was simply being kind, and wanting to enjoy her company.

'And will you wear a dress?' he asked almost plaintively. 'It's so long since I saw a woman in anything but trousers. I think it must be years.'

'If you're buying me dinner, it's the least I can do,' Clover said. 'And now, hadn't we better be going?'

Outside they fixed their skis and poled themselves along to the head of the trail.

'You go first,' Val said. 'I want to watch you, and who knows when I'll get the chance again. The trail's well marked, and it's only a red run. It's pretty bumpy though, so I should do it in short traverses. Can you see where you're going?'

He pointed out the line to Clover, and she nodded, pulled her goggles down, and pushed off. There was no one on the run to follow, but there had been skiers on it that day, and she could see their tracks quite clearly against the unmarked, billowy, off-piste snow. Let's go, she thought, remembering the slow morning and the slow afternoon ahead of her, let's really go. The morning's skiers had followed an easy line with long traverses round the moguls, but the wine was warming Clover's blood, and she went down hugging the fall-line, taking the shortest traverses and riding the moguls with a series of jet turns, her flexed knees taking up the unevenness.

The air whipped past her cheeks, the snow glittered in the sun like a carpet of diamond-dust and hissed under her skis. As she jetted curve and curve she felt the glory of speed, the power and suppleness of her own body, her mastery of the slope. Behind her, she heard Val give a yelp of glee and it spurred her on faster, the crystals spraying up beside her hard as sugar-grains.

All too soon it was over. The piste was running out, and she slowed herself with two wide loops and came to a showy stop a hundred yards from the lodge. Val skimmed to an equally showy stop beside her, and they pushed up their goggles and grinned exultantly at each other. Immediately Val flung his arms round her and hugged her, not an easy thing to do on skis.

'I can see who taught you, all right,' he said. 'You she-devil, springing that on me. I thought you'd take me down a nice lazy route. I'm too old for that kind of exercise.'

He wasn't even panting. She grinned at him affectionately. 'It was fun,' she said.

'It was,' he agreed. 'We must do it again some time – and get old George to come with us. I've an idea he doesn't get much fun out of life these days.'

SIX

VAL DROPPED her off at the hotel that afternoon at about five o'clock, and having left her boots, skis and poles in the store-room on the ground floor and put on her moon-boots instead, she strolled into the *stuberl* where Rose had told her they all met for a drink before going back to bathe before dinner. They were all there, all the Hot Max lehrers, plus Kris and three very pretty, over-made-up girls who were trying hard to look as though they belonged. Two seconds were sufficient to see they had been brought by Ernst, Wolf and Bruno respectively.

Rose greeted Clover noisily. 'Hey, there you are! Where've you been all day? You missed an absolutely super run down, didn't she, Wolf? We all skied down under the cables, and the piste was perfect. You never saw such perfect powder-snow. It's lovely early in the season, before people start coming down that way.'

Clover wriggled into the space Rose made for her between herself and Heinz. She turned to smile at Heinz, who was looking sulky.

'I wanted to have lunch with you,' he said. 'Where were you?'

Clover gave him a surprised look. She had not expected so much possessiveness, especially on the first day. She squeezed his hand under the table, and his sulkiness vanished instantly.

'I was with Val,' she said, and swung round on Rose, 'and don't say anything.'

'I wouldn't dream of it,' Rose said, showing a face of shining innocence. 'What were you doing with Val?'

'I had to sit in on his lessons,' Clover said, and the three girls went into fits of giggles. 'What's up?' Clover asked shortly.

'I was remembering my first lesson,' one of them said. 'Practically all I did was sit.'

They evidently thought she was one of the pupils, and not one of the lehrers. Never mind. She smiled indulgently and went on, 'He had a class on the nursery slopes in the morning, but he was teaching up the berg in the afternoon, so we lunched up there and then had the most fabulous run down from Rosenhof to the lodge. I've never skied so fast – it was out of this world!'

Rose looked cross. 'I might have known. I've never done that run – it's only been open a couple of weeks. When I agreed to be nice to you, I didn't know you were going to turn out to be a student of one-upmanship.'

Clover smiled sweetly. 'Never mind, dear, I'll take you one day.'

Rose punched her arm, and said, 'We're drinking *gluhwein*. Do you want some? I'll get you a mug.'

'Thanks, I'd love it.' Gluhwein was the favourite apres-ski drink there, and was a kind of hot spiced wine served in large earthenware mugs. It was warming and invigorating after a hard day's ski-ing, and in any circumstances was mildly and pleasantly intoxicating. The group was in a pleasant humour, and Heinz now had his arm round her shoulders and was rubbing his face, cat-like, against her cheek. The three girls were looking wistful, and Clover realised quite quickly that they had all liked the look of Heinz more than the men accompanying them.

'So where did you have lunch?' Heinz was asking her. Clover told him. 'That is a very nice place,' he said. 'And expensive. Val bought you lunch, did he?'

'Yes,' Clover said.

'You'll have to watch it, Clovy,' Rose said irrepressibly. 'Kris took me up there when I first arrived and now look what's become of me.'

'Clover is mine,' Heinz said suddenly and rather loudly.

Clover looked at him again in surprise, and said. 'You

73

surely aren't jealous of Val? He was only being nice.'

Heinz looked a little ashamed, and said. 'I wanted to have lunch with you. I haven't seen you all day.'

'Well, you're seeing me now,' Clover said.

Hugging her again, he said. 'Yes, and you will stay with me this evening, yes?'

'*Aber natürlich,*' she said to make him laugh, but inwardly she wondered at this display of jealousy and petulance. It was nice to know that he felt so strongly about her, but extraordinary and embarrassing to have him object to her activities away from him. The sooner he realised she was her own master the better. Also the sooner he was told she was going to dine with Val on Thursday the better, but if he was going to make a scene she didn't want it here in front of all these people, so she remained silent. Rose was asking her about the Rosenhof run, and she did her best to describe it.

After that the conversation became a typical apres-ski discussion of the day's incidents, the weather and the condition of the snow. Each of the lehrers had little anecdotes to tell of their classes, and they discussed various of the pupils that they all knew, the funny, the idiosyncratic, the promising, or the troublesome. The three guests had little to contribute, and were more out of it than ever, but following Heinz's example the other three lehrers had put their arms round them, so they looked contented.

It took them about an hour to talk themselves out, and then relaxed and warmed by the gluhwein they were ready to move. Rose yawned and stretched.

'I don't know about you, but I could do with a bath,' she said to no one in particular. 'I think we'd better make a move. Come on, Clover, let's set a good example. Anyway, if we don't get going there won't be time to bath and change before dinner, and you know if we don't have our snouts in the trough at seven exactly they take the swill away again.'

'Which would be a tragedy,' Clover said.

'It would be a tragedy to have to buy food when we're paid so little to start with. And besides I have to save all my wages for paying the Commandant's fines.'

'Why, what have you done?' Clover asked, startled.

'Nothing yet,' Rose said. 'But since all the things that are punishable according to George are the things I love to do, I've either got to make allowance for the fines or die of boredom.'

'Oh, Rose,' Clover said. Rose got up and walked bow-legged to the door.

'What was that memorable comment of Ian Fleming's in one of the James Bond books?' she said over her shoulder. ' "The knees are the Achilles' heel of all skiers." Except for beginners, of course. For them the B.T.M. generally turns out to be their Achilles knee.'

Rose wandered in to Clover's room while she was still dressing.

'I've just broken my eyeshadow stick in half. Can I borrow yours?'

'Help yourself. All my make-up's in that bag on the dresser,' Clover said.

Rose went over and rummaged, then said, 'My God, everything's so clean and tidy in here. You should see my bag – the tops seem to come off everything. You really are depressingly perfect, you know, Clover. I never could be clean and tidy, from childhood onwards.'

'I didn't use to be as a child,' Clover said, 'but I had to share a room in the first flat I lived in when I left home, and the other girl's mess depressed me so much that I got to be fanatically tidy out of sheer reaction. One never minds one's own mess, but other people's is squalid.'

'Hm. I know what you mean,' Rose said, then, abruptly, 'Val is nice, isn't he?'

'Very nice. Why?'

'No reason really. But Heinzie seemed to mind, didn't he?'

Clover turned round to look at Rose. 'Yes, that was odd. Is he generally like that? I was very surprised.'

'I don't know him much better than you do,' Rose said. 'I've only been here a couple of weeks longer than you. I haven't seen him like that before, but then I haven't seen him going out with a lehrer before, and none of the lehrers takes the guests very seriously, I'm sorry to say.'

'Yes, it does seem rather mean,' Clover said, thinking of the three girls looking uncomprehendingly from face to face.

'But he seems really smitten with you. I should be a bit careful. He's too close to home to have trouble with. Mind you, I wouldn't mind someone being as mad about me as that,' she said with a sigh. 'The people I go out with always seem to be overwhelmed with indifference.'

'Bowled over with inertia?'

'That sort of thing.'

'You choose the wrong sort of men.'

'They choose me. What I really need is a nice, steady, reliable older man.'

'Like Val?' Clover said idly, and was put out to see Rose blush and turn her face away.

'Oh, he wouldn't want me,' she said lightly. 'I'm too wild.'

'A wild rose is very beautiful,' Clover said.

'Yes, but their petals drop too quickly. No, those quiet types always go for the long-lasting, well-corseted garden rose. They're too sensible not to get value for their money.'

Clover wondered about that, but said no more. 'Are you ready?' she asked instead. 'Because it's nearly seven and I can hear the clank of buckets from below.'

The evening was much like the one before: dinner in the hotel restaurant, and then on to the disco. Ernst, Wolf and Bruno were still accompanied by their girls, and Kris and Rose had apparently made up their differences and were literally and metaphorically wrapped up in each other. The only difference was that it was not even midnight when Heinz pressed his mouth to Clover's ear and suggested that they went to bed. Rose and Kris made some loud and jolly remarks as the two of them said goodnight, which Clover answered with a derisive wave.

76

It was snowing when they got outside, and for a moment Clover was quite startled, having temporarily forgotten where she was. The flakes were large and soft-looking, and when she looked up at the sky she saw only a bewildering whiteness – the snow was coming down very heavily. She pondered on the strangeness of snow, on how surprisingly dry it was. If it was raining as heavily as this, they would not have been strolling through it – they would have been running, and drenched already.

'Tomorrow, what do you do?' Heinz asked suddenly as they headed for the annexe. Clover shrugged.

'I don't know yet. I suppose George will tell me tomorrow at the office.'

'Do you not go with Val?'

'I don't know,' Clover said again. He smiled to himself, and said. 'Then I think I ask the Commandant that you come to my lessons. You would like that?'

'Yes, I suppose so,' Clover said. It didn't matter to her what lessons she watched, if she was not to take a lesson herself.

'Then we can have lunch together, and ski down together in the afternoon.' Clover nodded, seeing his design now. He went on, 'Also, it will be good for you to watch my lesson. Val is a nice man, but as a skier –' He shrugged. With anyone else Clover would have been sure he was joking, but she wasn't yet terribly sure of Heinz. After all, those pictures and trophies all around his room . . .

In his room, Heinz wasted no time on talk, but took her at once in his arms and kissed her greedily. The smell of his skin and the softness of his lips worked on Clover at once, and everything she had thought about all day dropped away from her and there was nothing but sensation and the desire for his smooth body.

'It has seemed so long, such a long day,' Heinz murmured. 'I think about you all the time, beautiful Clover, and long for the night.'

They undressed each other, hands everywhere, and pressed against each other with a sigh of relief. It was just cool enough in Heinz's room to make it worth while snuggling down under the covers. Heinz wrapped his arms and legs round her, and nuzzled against her shoulder and breast, rubbing his face and hair against her skin in delight at the pure sensation. She had nothing to do but lie still and encompass his pleasure, as he created her own, but although she began languidly, almost drowsily, she was soon aroused by the unexpected intensity of his passion. It was, the distant part of her mind commented in surprise, as if he loved her.

They fell asleep at once afterwards, waking only enough to make themselves comfortable for sleep, but early in the morning, before it was even light, she woke simultaneously with him, and he smiled at her and murmured her name, and kissed her forehead and cheek, and soon they were making love again, warmly and sleepily like kittens in a basket. When she finally left him to bathe and dress in the morning it was with that glowing sensation that good love-making can bring; but she still had not told him about Thursday.

Whether as a result of Heinz's request or not, Clover was instructed to go with him and watch his lessons, and he accompanied her up to Karlspitze with a smile of satisfaction and what was almost a swagger in his walk. His lessons were quite different from Val's. His pupils were nine young women and two young men, and the young men got on with it without much help from Heinz, who instructed the female pupils with grave attention while they looked at him open-mouthed with admiration.

He certainly was a fine skier, but whether or not he was a good teacher, Clover found difficult to determine, since his pupils, while anxious for his help at every moment, were also anxious to excel and would agree to everything whether they understood or not. Several of them glanced at Clover with puzzlement, wondering who she was; and when Heinz from time to time turned to smile at her or addressed some obviously friendly remark to her, the looks changed to envy or even dislike. When at the end of the lesson they skied off together, some of the glances were pure homicide. No wonder Heinz thought well of himself, Clover thought with amusement as they went to lunch at the lodge. It would take a very strong character to resist a diet of pure adulation.

After the lessons, a number of them skied down together, traversing back and forth under the cable-car pylons until they came to the woods at the foot of the mountain when they swung aside and did a fast run over some very bumpy terrain to come in to the village at the opposite end to the baby slopes. They took off their skis at the side of the road and had a pleasant short walk in to leave their skis in the store-room before heading for the *stuberl,* gluhwein and the usual chat.

As they were turning into the *stuberl* Clover heard her name called, and turned to see Val leaning out of the window of his car beckoning to her. She excused herself to the party, ignoring Heinz's scowl, and went over to him. He greeted her with a friendly grin and patted her cheek.

'Lovely healthy colour you've got,' he said. 'Did you ski down?'

'Yes, under the cables, a group of us together. It was great fun.'

'It's an interesting run, but you need to be very careful. After a couple of days with the lehrers using it daily some of the guests will be coming down that way too, and the snow gets very thin. You can hit a rock or a root and break your leg. We always get one or two accidents there every season. I'll show you another way, a better run, next time we're up there together.'

'Thanks,' Clover said. 'I must say I'd like to get to see a bit more of the country.'

'Well, I'm your man,' Val said, and then gave a wry smile. 'Or at least, I wish I was. Which brings me to Thursday – it's still on, I hope?'

'Of course. A date's a date.'

'Good. Well, I was wondering if you'd mind very much if I invited George along too. He's been a bit low these last few days, and he could do with a change. He doesn't get out enough – spends a lot of his evening doing paperwork. Would you mind very much?'

'Not at all,' Clover said, thinking fast, 'except that he might feel a little awkward there being two men to only one woman. How would it be if we invited Rose along too?'

'Rose?' Val said doubtfully, 'I wouldn't have thought she'd come.'

'I'm sure she'd love to,' Clover said. 'She puts on a wild act, but I think secretly she's rather bored by the – what did you call them? Dead-beats?'

Val grinned. 'Don't tell them I said so. Well, by all means, if you think she'd like to come, do invite her, and I'll ask George, and we can have a foursome.'

'A fearsome word, foursome,' Clover smiled. 'I must go. I'll ask Rose. What time on Thursday?'

'I'll pick you up at the hotel at seven.'

As Clover slipped in to the space beside Heinz in the booth in the *stuberl* he put a possessive arm round her shoulders and said. 'What did Val want?'

Now for it, Clover thought. She told him about the outing on Thursday, but was glad to be able to say two others would be going as well, and Heinz, though he frowned, didn't seem to see it as a threat. Close to him, Clover looked again admiringly at his beautifully sculpted face, hot, wild-animal eyes, and silky hair, and felt the supple length of his body pressing against her, and knew that it was justification enough. She could never have had with him the kind of conversation she had just had with Val; but though she liked Val enormously, he didn't attract her physically as Heinz did. One man for one thing, and one man for another. She thought how lucky she was to be in the position of being able to have both. Perhaps it was unreasonable to expect to be able to have everything you wanted in the one person? But then, what happened when you wanted to settle down and marry? She sighed, and Rose looked across at her curiously.

'What?' she said. 'You've been looking mighty pensive for the last ten minutes, old pardner. What's the big sigh for?'

Clover looked demure. 'I was just thinking how silly it is to force women to be monogamous. One man simply isn't enough. I think we ought to march for polyandry.'

'Speak for yourself,' Rose retorted. 'I'm not marrying a parrot for anyone.'

'Come with me to the loo,' Clover said quietly. 'I've got something to ask you.'

They both got up, and Kris looked round as his arm was left vacant.

'I've always wondered why you women have to go to the bathroom in convoys,' he said. 'Is it because you want to discuss secrets?'

'Nothing so romantic,' Rose said. 'It's the world hair-brush shortage – we're rationed to one between two, nowadays.'

In the privacy of the loo, Clover put the invitation as casually as she could, but still not casually enough, for Rose, engaged in remaking-up her eyes, blushed a little and avoided looking at Clover as she elaborated on the idea.

'Val's such a kind person, he wants to give George a bit of fun,' Clover was saying, 'and I thought he might feel a bit out of things if the numbers weren't even. Will you come, Rosie? Please do. It'll be fun. You can make us all laugh.'

Rose, regarding her reflection, was suddenly serious. 'Yes, that's my role in life, the buffoon. I'm everyone's clown.' It wasn't said bitterly, only sadly, and Clover reached out and put her hand on Rose's shoulder affectionately.

'It isn't that, Rose. Everyone loves to laugh, and it's a great gift to be able to make people laugh. But people love you anyway.'

'Do they?' Rose said. 'I wonder. Still, having donned the mask to hide the broken heart, I can't very well take it off again, can I? Yes, all right, I'll come. I'd like to. Give Kris a chance to get off the leash – there are a couple of guests he feels he ought to take an interest in.'

'Ought to?'

'Keeping the customers satisfied, you know.' She grinned suddenly, back to her normal self. 'It's amazing the sacrifices these lads make in the line of duty, you know. Pure selflessness. VC jobs, every one. Why I've seen a lehrer chat up three different girls a week for a whole season without flinching.'

'No!' Clover opened her eyes wide with astonishment.

'S'fact,' Rose nodded. 'And if we don't get back in there, we'll find our dancing partners for the evening gone, so hop to it.'

On Thursday, Clover felt she had something to celebrate, because when she went to the office George was there waiting for her with a group of pupils.

'I think you should take a lesson today,' he said. 'I'm sorry you had to wait so long – I'd have given you a class yesterday but I didn't have time to arrange it. I've got a group of nine here that I've pulled out from other lessons, and since they're all here for two weeks you can take them right through. They're pretty much of a standard with each other. They've had three lessons on the nursery slopes, so you can take them up to Karlspitze today and start them on traversing with snowplough turns. You'll soon find out how much they know.'

'Thanks,' Clover said. 'I must admit I was getting bored.'

Unexpectedly, George smiled. 'I'm sure you were. I should have trusted you at the beginning, but the fact that I didn't is due to old habit, and no reflection on you. I apologise.'

'No need,' Clover said, surprised. 'You have to be careful. So where's this class of mine?'

George introduced her to the group, seven men and two women, all young, in their late teens or early twenties. Amongst them, Clover noticed two men from Val's beginners' class, and she gave them a smile of recognition. The composition of the group amused her, and she wondered if the men had been 'pulled out' of largely

82

female classes with the male lehrers. However, they looked at her with interest and without hostility, so she felt no qualms as she led her very first group down to the lifts.

She travelled up on the sesselbahn with one of the girls, whose name was Marilyn, and who was about eighteen, very pretty, and a great talker.

'I was in Kris's class,' she told Clover, 'but I didn't like him very much. He made me nervous – he was always so loud and, sort of, flirty – I don't know really. Whenever he came near me I got all flustered and fell over, and that made it worse.'

It gave Clover the hint that the people she had been given had been pulled out of their classes because for one reason or another they weren't getting on with their lehrers, and for a moment she wondered whether she had a group of trouble-makers. But then she thought of big, loud Kris – 'flirty' was not exactly the way she would have described him but she knew what Marilyn meant – and decided that in any group of people there would always be one or two who just didn't get on together.

Up at the lodge, she gathered her class together, supervised the putting on of the skis, and then sought out an empty patch of the field to start the lesson.

'Now today we're going to start off with traversing,' she said. 'This is what you do when you want to cross a slope diagonally instead of going straight down it, and since you'll be crossing most slopes diagonally for most of your ski-ing life, you can see that it's a very important thing to learn and to be able to do comfortably.'

She demonstrated the basic position, explained about edging the skis uphill, and showed them the compensatory leaning position of the body.

'It may sound crazy to you to say that you lean away from the slope.'

'Sounds bloody suicidal,' one of the young men interrupted, and there was laughter. Clover smiled, glad they were relaxing.

'But in fact you'll find it comes perfectly naturally when you come to do it. Your body then forms what we call a ''comma'' shape, and you'll find that as your uphill shoulder turns away from the slope,' she demonstrated, 'your uphill ski automatically moves a little ahead of the other one. And that's your basic traverse position. Now let's try it here on the flat first.'

She went round, correcting their positions and answering their queries, and then they went on the 'meat hook' drag up to the top of the first slope, which was very gentle, and tried traversing there. She soon began to get a feel of the class, the good ones, the competent ones, and those who were never going to get very far. She picked out the two possible trouble-makers – the girl Marilyn who was slope-shy, and one of the boys, a South African in his early twenties with a loud mouth and a propensity to show off – his name was Piet. The others she found pleasant and friendly, there to learn and to enjoy themselves.

By the end of the lesson they were all traversing reasonably easily to left and right, and were beginning to join the traverses together into loops with snowplough turns. At twelve o'clock, they stopped and returned to the lodge, all pretty well satisfied with their progress. Clover left them and joined Heinz and Wolf.

In the afternoon they continued, and when they stopped at four she told them that the next day they could go on to swing turns, which would mean that they could move continuously across the fall-line in one motion. She said good night to them, and hurried ahead to the lift to travel down from the sunlit peak to the shadowed valley. She wanted to avoid going down with Heinz, feeling sure he would be unable to prevent himself from commenting on his lonely evening to come.

SEVEN

It was lovely to put on a dress again, and Clover felt grateful to Val for giving her the chance, so she started off the evening in the right frame of mind, prepared the enjoy herself. She heard Rose come in while she was dressing and called to her.

'God, are you ready already? How did you get back so fast?' Rose asked putting her head round the door.

'I dashed off straight away and came down in the lift. I didn't want to get caught talking.'

'Very wise. That's what kept me, of course. I'll still be talking when they come to bury me.'

'What are you wearing?'

'Well, not a dress anyway – I haven't got one. I suppose it'll be a smart do?'

'No idea. Val asked me to dress up, so I did. Mostly to cheer him up, I think.'

'Oh! In that case – I suppose a trouser suit will do? If I'd known, I could have gone out and got something. I suppose you haven't got a dress to lend me?'

Clover did not smile at this transparency. 'No, I've only got the one. A trouser suit will do very nicely, I'm sure. You've got the kind of beauty that looks good in anything.'

Rose snorted at that and went away to bathe and change, and was ready by half past six, when she came knocking on Clover's door.

'Come on, I want to have a drink before they arrive. I'm as nervous as a cripple on an ice rink.'

'I can't think why,' Clover said. 'You do look nice – that

colour really suits you.' Rose's trouser suit was of an eau-de-nil colour which not only set off her red-gold hair but also her suntan. 'Besides, I want to avoid any of the others, so maybe a drink isn't the best idea.'

'Don't worry, they're all safe in their rooms or in the bathroom. I've been listening behind my door for the last ten minutes. The safest place to be is down in the main bar – they won't come in there until seven, and we'll be gone by then, I hope.'

Clover gave in and went down to the bar with her, and observed that Rose really was nervous, for she ordered a large vodka martini, and sank half of it before Clover had got her own gin-and-tonic to her lips. By the time Val arrived at 6.55 she was halfway down a second, but seemed to be more relaxed.

'Hello – I hope I haven't kept you waiting,' Val said when he saw them at the bar.

'No, you're early,' Clover said. 'We were just warming up.'

'You both look stunning,' Val said appreciatively. 'It's so nice to see people not wearing ski clothes for a change.'

'Ditto, ditto,' Clover said. Val was wearing a dark brown velvet suit that made him look very distinguished. He smiled at her compliment, but his eyes kept wandering back to Rose, who was gulping down the rest of her drink.

'There's no hurry,' he said, afraid she would choke herself.

'Oh, yes there is,' she said. 'I want to get out of here before the others come down and start laughing.'

'Well, the car's outside. Shall we go?'

The car was parked just outside with the lights on and George in the back, and Clover walked ahead and planted herself by the back door so that Rose had to sit in front with Val. Val opened the doors and Clover slid in beside George, who moved over to make room for her saying, 'You're very punctual.'

'I always am,' Clover replied.

'It's a trait George values above all others,' Val commented, getting into the driver's seat. 'He even fines himself if he's late waking up.'

'Oh, it's going to be one of *those* evenings, is it?' George said. Val grinned at him in the driving mirror as he drove off.

'I sincerely hope so.'

They drove out on to the main road which ran along beside the river. It was snowing lightly, and Clover gazed fascinated at the white flakes disappearing into the black water.

'You can almost hear them hissing,' she observed. George looked too, and then, encouraged by her friendly tone of voice, opened conversation.

'How did your first lesson go?' he asked her.

'Well enough,' she said. 'No problems, though I can see where they'll arise. You slipped a joker into my hand, didn't you?'

'Who's that?'

'The South African, Piet. The show-off.'

'Ah, you spotted the deliberate mistake,' George said. 'I thought you'd want something a little challenging, a woman of your talents. I had to move him on, actually, before there was real trouble. As you probably noticed, he was in your boy Heinz's class, and they were all set for pistols in the library.'

'Not *my* boy,' Clover objected, though without great force. She didn't want a quarrel on that of all topics.

'Well, your mountebank then,' George corrected himself indifferently while Rose gave a snort of laughter from the front.

'I don't think it was the noun she was objecting to, but the pronoun,' Val said.

'It always puzzles me what you women see in him,' George said rather peevishly. 'Year after year it's the same.'

'You have to admit,' Rose said, 'that he's very decorative.'

George pretended to consider. 'Yes, that's true. And he has wonderfully even teeth, though he smiles too much for my liking.'

'You have remarkably even teeth yourself,' Clover said, hoping to deflect him.

'Ah, you noticed,' he said, turning to her in the dark and displaying them for a change. 'I may not smile very often, but I chew with real elegance.'

Clover laughed, and felt him relax. The car was small, and she was very aware of his nearness, and when the car went round a bend she allowed herself to be swayed against him, and found that he did not move away. It gave her food for thought on the short drive. Perhaps Val was playing the same game as she was.

The restaurant when they reached it was bright with lights, and inside noisy with talk and music. There was a live band playing, a mixture of modern and traditional music, and there seemed to be a great many German tourists dining there who wanted to sing along with the band. As they were shown to their table, Clover was saved from being made to feel greatly inferior by the richness of the other diners' clothes and jewels, by the consoling realisation that she and her companions were the youngest and handsomest people there. They sat down, and she found herself beside Val and opposite George, facing outwards into the restaurant.

The menus were huge, and covered just about every nationality the restaurant was likely to play host to. After much hesitation, Clover chose poached salmon to start with, and George wrinkled up his nose.

'It'll be deep frozen,' he said. 'You're miles from the sea here.'

'In Edinburgh, where I used to live,' Clover said, 'they had their own fishing fleet, and still all the fish you could buy was deep frozen. It seems to be one of the obscure rules of economics that the stuff you grow yourself has to be sent abroad so that you can eat other people's stale produce and they can eat yours.'

'Where I come from,' George said, 'I could get you real salmon, caught that very day.'

'And it probably would be poached, too,' Val remarked. 'But still, forbidden fruits and all that.'

'I hope that isn't a loaded remark,' Rose said.

'What part of Scotland do you come from?' Clover wanted to know.

'Inverness,' George said. 'I grew up on the slopes at Aviemore. That's how I first got interested, of course.'

'And do you never want to go back?' Clover asked, and wished she hadn't, for his face shut down fractionally.

'All the time,' he said as if indifferently. 'But it isn't a possibility.' He intended that to be the end of that, but Rose either didn't pick up, or ignored, the tone of voice.

'Why? I wouldn't stay away if I wanted to go back.'

'It wouldn't be possible to earn a living over there. The only thing I know how to do is ski.'

Val and Clover exchanged a glance, and Val broke in boisterously, 'That's a monstrous lie, and he's playing shamelessly on your sympathies, girls. God, I wish I had your technique, George. I have to rely on picking up fallen beginners and rubbing their bruises, but he's got so many notches on his poles they threaten to give way under him.'

George picked up the cue. 'Ah, but I'm still on my first poles. You've turned the clock back three times.'

'He's mocking my extreme age, you see, girls,' Val said cheerfully. 'Still you must admit I'm wonderful for an old man.'

'You're not old,' Rose protested loyally, and he patted her on the head.

'I'm the oldest skier I know. I'm the Herbert von Karajan of the slopes. I've got so many prostheses that when I go through the scanners at airports they have to take me to pieces and reassemble me on the plane. When they finally pay out on my life insurance, they'll make a deduction for my value as scrap.'

There were no more awkward moments after that, and the meal went along merrily. Clover had, after her fish, the best chicken Kiev she had ever tasted, and the others ordered things with garlic in them to be companionable. They had a very good white Burgundy with the main course, and when it came to dessert Val, who seemed to have very good ideas about entertainment, said, 'How

89

about having a bottle of champagne with the pudding? After all, it is a celebration.'

Rose looked languid. 'My dear, fancy thinking it has to be a celebration before you can drink champagne! Personally, I always have it as an aperitif, but better late than never.'

George managed to look even more languid and said in his best Duthie Park drawl, 'How I agree, darling. But let's order a bottle anyway – I haven't had any since breakfast.'

Val winked at Clover before turning to look for the waiter, but she wasn't able to give her return wink her full attention, since she was pondering the problem of whether George's pressure on her lower leg under the table was accidental or not. The champagne came, and did its job.

'I wonder why the bubbles are so very festive,' she said lifting her glass. 'Or is it all force of association?'

'Yes and no,' Rose said, giving the question the answer it deserved. For dessert, they all had the chef's special, which turned out to be a very soft, very tangy lemon mousse on a crisp pastry base, covered in whipped cream. Then they had coffee served, and another bottle of champagne instead of liqueurs, and they lingered, listening to the music and watching the dancing. Val asked Clover if she wanted to dance, but she refused, saying she felt too full for exercise. The truth was that she had spent so much time in the last few days dancing with Heinz that she didn't want to spoil the evening by association.

They were all very relaxed and happy with one another, and the happiness and the drink were beginning to make Clover sleepy when finally George said, 'I think we'd better be making a move, don't you, Val? After all, we've all got a heavy day in front of us tomorrow.'

When they got outside, the snow had stopped, the sky had cleared, and it was freezing hard. The girls gasped at the cold air, and any sleepiness was gone instantly. Clover looked up at the sky, black as deep water and pitted with a million stars like sugar frosting.

'What a night! I don't know if it's the champagne or what, but suddenly I feel as if I could jump over a mountain,' Clover said mistily.

''I know what you mean,' Rose said, turning a sparkling face to her. 'What a pity we have to go home.'

The two men looked doubtfully at each other, and Val said, 'Well, I suppose we could go and dance somewhere –'

'Oh, not dancing,' Clover said. 'I've had enough of dancing. No, I know we have to go home. It was only an idle wish.'

They piled into the car and began the drive back, but her restlessness had communicated itself even to George, and she knew they were all feeling they didn't want the evening to end. To prolong matters, Val turned off the main road early to come into the village by the back road, and it was as well he did, for it took him past the open-air tennis courts which had been flooded and frozen for the winter to make an open-air skating rink. As they reached it, they heard even through the engine noise the sound of waltz-music; there were floodlights playing on the ice itself, and the trees all around had been decorated with coloured fairy-lights.

'Oh, look – skating!' Clover cried out. She did not need to say anything more. Val pulled in to the side of the road, and they all looked at one another hopefully.

'My skates are back at the hotel,' Clover said.

'Mine too,' George said.

'They hire them here,' Val said. 'In the pavilion.'

Clover looked at George. 'I'd sooner have my own,' she said apologetically. He nodded, understanding.

'Me too. Look, Val and Rose can stay here and get themselves fitted out, and I'll drive you back to the hotel, drop you off, collect my skates, and pick you up on the way back. It will only take ten minutes. How about it?'

Clover did not need any urging, and if Rose had any objections they were smothered by Val who fairly shoved her out of the car to let George take the driving seat before he changed his mind and realised what the time was. Dropped off at the hotel, Clover raced upstairs and, knowing she was a quick dresser, tore off her clothes and put on her skating dress and tights, which were red, and her ski-ing anorak and woolly hat. Then she grabbed her skates and raced down again, to find George waiting just outside in the car with the engine running.

'You changed,' he said, looking her up and down. 'You didn't need to – nobody bothers here.'

'I can't bear skating with my legs muffled up,' Clover excused herself. 'I'm not used to it.'

'Well, you certainly look very smart,' he said. 'You'll put us all to shame.'

Clover felt a little put out at that, wondering whether she was going to look ludicrously over-dressed – or under-dressed might be the more appropriate expression. She didn't remember seeing anyone else in skating dress there. But she consoled herself with the fact that what she had said was at least partly true – she did hate skating in a long skirt, or even trousers.

When they got back to the tennis courts, they quite soon discovered Rose and Val sitting on one of the spectators' benches fitting on their hired skates, which were brown and rather battered.

'God knows what this will do to your suit,' Rose was saying cheerfully. 'If you fall you'll mark horribly. Oh, here they are – I say, Cloves, what are you trying to do to my morale? As it is, I'm only just capable of staying upright.'

'I'm showing off,' Clover said, sitting beside her and pulling off her shoes. 'There has to be something in this world I'm better at than you.'

'Well, you've hit on the right way to humiliate me,' Rose said gloomily. 'How am I ever going to catch my man with you to point up the contrast.'

'Never mind, Rose,' Val said. 'I'm no skater either. We can totter down together.'

'And sleep together at the foot,' George murmured. Clover caught the allusion and laughed at him. The tennis courts were arranged in two pairs, and the dividing wire-netting between them had been taken down, so that the flooded area made a rink of very decent proportions. The music was taped and being played over a loudspeaker, and

92

had evidently been chosen specifically, for it contained a great number of waltzes and other strict-tempo dances suitable for skating; 'The Skater's Waltz' seemed to come round fairly frequently. The lights were wonderful against the velvety darkness of the sky beyond them, and the voices and laughter of the skaters rang hollowly on the frosty air. Her skates fixed, Clover got to her feet, feeling the energy – probably mostly spurious her mind told her – surging through her blood.

'Come on, I can't wait,' she said. The four of them stepped on to the ice together – Rose and Val with pawky carefulness, George with a fair amount of assurance, and Clover excitedly. Laughing, she swung round backwards and held her hands out to George.

'You beastly show-off! I hope you fall over!' Rose shouted furiously.

'Ah, but it doesn't matter if I do,' she called back gleefully. 'I'm dressed for it.'

'I must say, you're worth looking at,' George said. 'I think you were right to change – you look so much more comfortable.' His grey wool trousers and woollen-tweed bomber-jacket were much too smart to be skating in, but he skated pretty well, as neatly as he seemed to do everything. Rose, like most skiers, could stay upright and get about, but without any great skill; Val was wobbling and wavering all over the place. George, catching up with Clover and skating along beside her, said, 'Val's a clown – he can skate better than me. He's putting on a pretty good act.'

'You can see why,' Clover said.

'Oh yes – when he loses his balance he can grab hold of Rose.'

'Do you mind?' Clover asked curiously. George's face was expressionless.

'Why should I mind? It's you who should mind.'

'Why on earth me?' Clover asked, astonished.

'Well, it was you he asked out for the evening,' George said.

'But it doesn't matter. He asked all three of us, if it

93

comes to that. We're just –'

'Good friends?' George finished for her. She had to laugh at that, and after a moment he smiled too.

'That's better,' she said. 'Smiling suits you – you should do it more often.' She did a three-turn so that she could skate backwards in front of George and hold out her hands to him. Automatically her body was moving in time to the music. It was so nice to be once again in complete mastery, after a week in which she had been, however slightly, in an alien environment.

'You really skate very well,' George said, and Clover felt a tingle of excitement at his tone of admiration.

'So do you,' she said.

'I skate adequately, but I'm not graceful the way you are. You're like a bird, skimming along there.'

'Listen,' Clover said, 'they're playing my favourite waltz!'

' "The Belle of the Ball" '?' George said, after listening to a bar or two.

'Yes – don't you feel it, it's so lovely to dance to, so smooth and sweeping. Come, dance with me – you can waltz, can't you?'

'I'm rusty,' he said, but all the same he took her hands and swung her round beside him. Two forward strokes and then Clover made the three-turn that put her into his arms in the pairs position. A little stiffly at first, but with increasing confidence, George guided her through the crowds of skaters, his small, careful steps extending as the joy of the movement worked on him. No one else had been dancing, but Clover's scarlet skating-dress and their increasing speed and grace worked on the other skaters so that the beginners and fallers gradually moved to the sides of the rink, and other couples began to join George and Clover as the space in the centre cleared.

'Everyone's looking at you,' George said, smiling down at her as he gripped her tighter for the quadruple-turn at the foot of the rink.

'At us,' Clover said wickedly, looking up into his eyes. 'Don't we make a lovely couple?'

For a moment he looked down at her, his face very close. 'I wish we did,' he said quietly. Clover's mouth dried as she felt something far inside her unlocking. Then spun her extra hard, and moved even faster down the long side, passing all the other dancers with two swooping half circles. She knew from the feeling of his body he had forgotten himself, which is the best way to skate well. He was supple and strong and relaxed, his arm lightly braced about her waist, his hand firm and dry in her grip, his feet passing between her tracks as easily as if they had been ice-dancing together all their lives. 'The Belle of the Ball' ended and 'The Skater's Waltz' came on after it and they went on dancing. They passed Val and Rose, doing a very slow prelim waltz along the side of the rink, and Val grinned at them as they passed and gave a thumbs-up to Clover. Now there were other dancers in skating-dress, a girl in royal-blue trimmed with fur and two lads in the one-piece stretch suits that men wore nowadays. Presumably they had thought it worthwhile, now there was proper dancing, to go back and change.

After another dance, they had slowed down considerably, and George spun Clover into a corner and said, 'I need a rest. And so do you.'

'I felt as if I could go on for ever,' she said ecstatically, 'But I know what you mean.' Her legs were trembling, she discovered, and she was glad to drop down on to a bench.

Val came to a showy stop beside them, forgetting himself for a moment, and said, 'They're selling hot chocolate over there. Shall we go and get some?'

Large urns had been set up at one end of the pavilion veranda, and the four of them went over there and bought mugs of hot chocolate and the little spicy biscuits that Germans eat at Christmas. They cupped their hands around the mugs and watched the skaters through the steam.

'See what you've started,' Rose said to Clover, nodding at the rink. 'It's all very well, but it's not fair on the poor old beginners.'

'Never mind,' Val said. 'When we've finished our drinks

we can change over, and you can go with George while Clover takes me. It's wonderful the difference skating with someone who can do it makes. I wouldn't be surprised if I didn't find a great improvement in my style.'

Back on the ice, he took Clover in his arms and whirled away in a foxtrot, making several mistakes but getting around them quite nimbly.

'You old fraud,' Clover said to him. 'I saw you fooling about. George says you can skate better than he can.'

'But I put up a good show, didn't I?' he grinned, unrepentant. 'And all's fair in love and war, so they say.'

'So which is it with you?'

'Which is it with you?' he countered quickly. They exchanged a look of understanding.

'I thought the two of us were doing a rescue job,' Clover said.

'Maybe it started that way,' Val said, and left it at that. They did a turn or two, and then Clover really was tired, the alcohol-induced energy having worn itself out.

'You'd better go home to bed, or you'll be fit for nothing in the morning,' Val said, feeling her flagging.

'I don' wanna,' she whined convincingly, and he took her firmly by the elbow and steered her to the side. Next time round George and Rose joined them, and the two men exchanged glances.

'Best get these two slips of girls back to their cots,' George said.

Rose rubbed her cheek against George's shoulder in what Clover recognised with horror as a fair imitation of Heinz, and said, 'Why not get us back to your cots?'

'None of that,' George said firmly, and Clover saw with relief he hadn't recognised the imitation. 'You need your beauty sleep. It'll be a long day tomorrow.'

'Twenty-four hours, same as today,' Rose objected, and when he shook her a little she fluttered her eyelashes and cooed, 'Ooh, you are masterful!' They changed out of their skates and walked back to the hotel in a companionable silence. Rose and Val, Clover noticed out of the corner of her eye, were holding hands, and she felt so at ease with George that they might have been within inches of holding hands too, though in fact both of them were swinging their skates instead. At the hotel door they paused and looked at each other, happy with the evening, reluctant that it should end, and not knowing quite how to say good night.

'You know, I was thinking –' George began, but got no further, for at that moment Heinz came round the corner from the hotel and broke in on their group.

'Oh, there you are, Clover,' he said loudly. 'It is very late – I thought you would have been back before this. I have been two times to your room to see, and two times back to the *stuberl. Ganz alein – schade, ne?'*

He put his arm clumsily round her shoulders, and though she pushed his arm away crossly, the damage was done. The atmosphere between the four of them was shattered. George drew back, physically as well as metaphorically.

'I'll say good night now,' George said. 'I can see you are in good hands. Val, do you realise you've left the car back at the tennis courts. I'll come with you to fetch it, and you can give me a lift home. Good night, Rose. Thanks for a pleasant evening.'

He turned on his heel and walked away, and Val gave a comical shrug, patted Rose's hand, and went off in pursuit.

'What is the matter with the ·Commandant?' Heinz asked loudly of no one in particular.

'You should know,' Clover snapped. He spread his hands.

'Me? Why should I know?' He looked genuinely innocent and injured, and Clover could not decide whether he knew or not. In any case, it was too late now. Rose looked at her and shrugged.

'He'll live,' she said. 'Come on, let's get to bed.'

Heinz cheered up at that, but Clover said, 'Yes, bed – and tonight, Heinzie my child, *ganz alein.* I need the sleep.' Which seemed to cover the situation either way.

EIGHT

THE RACES held on Friday afternoon were mainly for those whose holiday finished on the Saturday, but several others joined in for fun. The course was designed so that anyone who had mastered the basic traverse and schuss positions could get down it, and the competitors were timed, the fastest winning. There was an overall prize, and prizes for each lehrer's class.

'Actually,' Rose told Clover beforehand, 'the whole thing's incredibly foxy, because the class prizes are medals – you know, *à la* Olympics, a gold, silver and bronze – and everyone who goes in for the damned race at all gets at least a tin medal, so it isn't worth a button to win. Mind you, it's amazing how competitive some of these birds get.'

'What are the medals made of?' Clover wanted to know.

'Some kind of thin foil, I think. They pin on with safety pins, anyway. My own theory is that George sits up all night cutting them out of milk bottle tops.'

It was a pleasant afternoon, however, and there was a very festive feeling about the whole thing. The course was laid out during lunch-time by all the lehrers working together, and it was the first time Clover met those of the German school. There were no classes in the afternoon, so those guests who weren't competing became spectators and collected in bunches at various points along the course. It took Clover some minutes to work out that they were gathering around the lehrer of their predilection.

Clover and Rose were put at the finishing line. All the lehrers were positioned somewhere along the course to supervise and to be on hand in case of accident, and

98

they were equipped with walkie-talkie sets for inter-communication.

'George runs it like a military operation,' Rose grumbled. 'That's why we're stuck here with nothing to do – don't let the girls join in, they'll spoil it.'

Clover didn't mind being at the finishing line – it was more interesting than being halfway up the mountain all afternoon, and the loos and cafés were within striking distance. Heinz had what she discovered was his usual job right at the top, of starter; George was at the bottom organising, and Val was at the finish with the flag and stop-watch. Clover suspected they had been kept at the bottom because George and Val were there, but she didn't say so to Rose.

Clover was talking to a group of her pupils late in the afternoon when Rose, who had been hanging around Val looking, to Clover, rather wistful, came over to her.

'Val says the last one's on his way down,' she said. 'Let's push off and get a sauna at the hotel. I'm bloody cold with all this hanging around.'

'Won't we be needed?' Clover asked. Rose shrugged.

'If they won't let us play, why should we have to help clear up? Someone's got to collect the flags, pick up the corpses, sweep the dismembered limbs off the piste, and find some wet girl's goggles that she thinks she lost just after flag six, but we haven't got our skis on anyway. Come on – with a bit of luck we'll have the sauna to ourselves.'

They did. It wasn't a very large sauna – it had room for no more than eight people sitting, so it was just pleasant for two lying down. Rose, complaining of the cold, climbed up on to the top bench and stretched out, while Clover sat on the bottom bench and examined her toes.

'Ah, this is better,' Rose sighed. 'What my body must think – from Siberia to the Mojave in one leap! Why ever did God invent snow – nasty cold wet stuff.'

'How did your pupils do in the race?' Clover asked. Rose snorted.

'Don't ask. I'm shamed for ever. But it isn't my fault –

they always give me the absolute hopelesses when they share out the pupils. I suppose they reckon they won't learn anything anyway, so they might as well give them to someone who can't teach them anything to begin with.'

'Surely that's not right,' Clover said. 'It must be a compliment to you to give you the people nobody else could do anything with?'

'A noble try, my girl, but wide of the mark,' Rose said. 'The *obersturmbahnführer* has got the measure of me. How did your pupils get on?'

'I only had two in it,' Clover said. 'That poor little beast Marilyn, who's going home tomorrow – I'm glad for her sake she is, because another week would probably kill her – and Piet, the walking accident black spot.'

'And how did they do?'

'Both fell over, one at the first gate and one at the last.'

'I like your class,' Rose said, rolling over on to her front to look down at Clover. 'I got chatting to them this afternoon while you were off communing with nature. I can see why you were given them. Now, if I'd been given a bunch like that I wouldn't have to chase after lehrers.'

'Did you get any offers, then?'

'Only one fiver and two Barclay Cards, but it was a start.'

'Oh, Rose! And how is your particular lehrer?'

'Don't ask,' Rose said. Clover stretched out on her back and looked up at the other girl.

'Are you really keen on Val?' she asked abruptly.

'Keen? What a silly word,' Rose said softly. 'I don't know for sure, but I think I'm crazy about him.'

'Only think?'

'How can I tell? After a difficult start, our relationship proceeds with all the smoothness of a bull rhinoceros being eased through a Chinese laundry press. In any case, what would he want with me? If he's managed without a woman all these years, he's hardly likely to break his duck with a fool like me, is he?'

'I don't see why not. He's probably never met anyone like you before. *Nil desperandum*, kid.'

'I'd even go out with him, I'm that desperate.'

'Who?'

'Neil Desperandum.'

'What we need is a plan,' Clover said. Rose raised an eyebrow.

'We? Clover, my child, is that a blush I spy stealing across your velvet cheek? Can it be that the honey-bee of love has crept unawares up your foxglove bell? Of course, I know Heinz has got the build for a Lorelei, and the long hair, but I can't see him crouching on a rock singing as you ski past on your way home to tea. I dare say it isn't only sitting on radiators that gives you piles.'

Clover ignored all this. 'What I was thinking is that it might be easier and less obvious to get you together with Val if we made up another foursome.'

'Cunning little vixen, you,' Rose said. 'Here, move over, I'm coming down. I can't think up there, with the blood vessels expanding like McDonalds' hamburger chain all over ma boady, as George would say.'

'He wouldn't,' Clover said at once. 'His accent, if he can be said to have one, is educated Aberdeen.'

'Sounds like a circus act — Tex Rotter, and his Educated Aberdeen. So it is him you're after then. I'm afraid I have to warn you, you're flogging a dead horse. He's vowed his virginity to the god of organisation.'

'We'll see.'

'She said enigmatically.'

'At least, you'd better let me handle negotiations. You're about as subtle as a soap-powder advert.'

The party that night was held in the main restaurant-bar area of the Hotel Maximillian. A platform had been set up at one end, and at eight o'clock the lehrers all gathered in their best bibs and tuckers. George gave each of them a list of his class members with their times over the competition course and their order. Seeing this, Clover realised how much work he had to do in organising these things. She thought it probable that he, with whatever helpers he had, had skipped dinner to have these lists ready.

When he judged that the guests had all arrived he made a

short speech telling them what was to happen, hoping they had all enjoyed themselves, and thanking them for coming. Rose snorted rather loudly at that point and had to blow her nose to cover up for it.

Then each of the lehrers stood up in turn and came to the front of the platform to read out his class list, give the times, and present the medals, gold, silver and bronze for the first, second and third and tin for the rest. There was much joking and chaffing of the pupils, and Ernst, when he gave out his prizes, insisted on kissing each of his female pupils thoroughly and so lengthily that the other lehrers began to join in the barracking. Heinz was the exception to the rule, and gave out his class's medals with a seemly gravity, while his young ladies accepted them with upraised, adoring eyes.

'It's like a blooming confirmation class,' Rose commented to Clover, 'except that Bishop Heinz doesn't lay on his hands. If he did, they'd be coming up twice each.'

'I don't know how he does it,' Kris said. 'I never manage to get more than one or two adoring me. I've never had the whole class looking at me like that.'

'Personality,' Clover said curtly. 'Or lack of it.'

'Who, and which?' Kris asked.

'Work it out for yourself,' Clover smiled sweetly .

Clover had only two names to call, of course, and was amused to find George had provided her with a gold and a silver medal. She was pleased to be able to pin the silver on Marilyn who, ironically, had the slowest time of the whole competition. When it came to pinning the gold on Piet, his smug expression and swaggering gait infuriated her, and when he offered to kiss her as well, she only just restrained herself from pinning the medal right through into his skin.

'You're going home tomorrow, of course,' she said. He looked surprised.

'No, I've got another week,' he said. 'I thought you knew.'

'Pity,' she murmured just low enough for him not to be sure she had actually said it.

After the presentations, the lehrers vacated the stage and a band took their place. George made a quick round of the lehrers, murmuring something to each of them. When he reached Rose and Clover they discovered what it was.

'Don't stand around in groups tonight, please. Mix with the guests. It's their night tonight. I don't want to see you lehrers dancing with each other.'

Rose threw a smart GI salute. 'Okay, cherub, if that's what you want. I think it's very brave of you to lend out your women-folk like that.'

George stopped looking harassed for a fraction of a second to say, 'Well, we might take you back later on. Depends how the evening goes,' before passing on. Heinz came over to them as soon as George had gone.

'The Commandant has said we must not dance together,' he complained. 'He has said I must dance with my pupils.'

'Poor you,' Clover said, not without irony. Rose looked stern.

'I should think so to. What you have to realise, my boy, is that love is not just a pleasure – it's a responsibility; especially where you have induced adoration. Duty and freedom are the obverse and reverse of the same coin. The one is implicit in the other.'

'Please?' said Heinz. Rose ruffled his hair.

'Skip it, Curly. Go and kootch with your nuns.' Heinz did not look reassured. He was afraid something was going on that he didn't know about. He looked at Clover.

'But you will wait for me?' he said plaintively. 'Afterwards, you will with me?'

'Oh yes, I will with you all right,' Clover said, touched that he should want her so much, when there was so much competition.

'Amazing, isn't it,' Rose said when he had gone. 'How suggestive broken English can be. "You will with me?" I tell you what, though, Clovettes, that boy has fallen harder for you than either of us would have thought. Maybe the bit of discreet rivalry was good for him. I don't suppose he's ever had to face any before.'

Clover watched him talking to one of his pupils. 'He really is astonishingly attractive,' she said dreamily.

'Dost thou affect him?' Rose asked. 'No, don't answer. He *is* attractive, but one can't really take him seriously, can one? Come on, I can see the master's beady eye on us – we'd better circulate. I must say it's at times like these I envy you your class. It won't be any pleasure to me dancing with mine.'

'You can have some of mine. Even an experienced girl like me can't get through nine men in three hours.'

Being separated from Clover for two evenings seemed to have worked on Heinz, for he could barely keep his hands off her until they were in his room, and he made love to her all night long with such passion and energy that Clover was left stunned.

'It's like being in bed with a leopard,' she murmured early in the morning when he had woken her from sleep to make love again. He lay across her, spent for the moment, his lips drawn back from his beautiful teeth as he panted for breath. Clover stroked his hard back and his smooth flanks admiringly as she lay back against the pillows. Her body felt wonderful, relaxed and tingling and loved. He made her feel beautiful in a way that Joe never had, and though she did not love him – there was no question of it – she was grateful to him, felt great affection for him, and something else, a kind of wondering pride in the possession of him.

'You too,' he said, pushing himself up to look at her. 'You are a leopard too. Look, look at us – we are beautiful together, *nicht wahr?*'

He pulled her into a sitting position and put an arm round her and directed her gaze towards the mirror that now reflected them both. Their glowing, golden bodies folded softly together, their ruffled hair and flushed, sleepy faces did make a lovely picture.

'I love you,' Heinz said in a voice that lost confidence between the beginning and the end even of such a short sentence. Clover could say nothing in return, but she remembered Rose's half-mocking words of the night before. Though she had not asked for Heinz's love, it still conferred a kind of responsibility on her.

'We may not be a couple,' she said at last, 'but I suppose we are at least a pair.' And Heinz, instead of saying 'please?', kissed her again and pressed her back down amongst the pillows.

Rose caught Clover on her way to the bathroom on Saturday morning and said, 'I'm depressed. I need to spend some money. How about coming into Innsbruck with me? We can look at the shops and have lunch and sightsee or something. Maybe do a flick or something in the evening. What say?'

'We wouldn't be allowed to stay out all evening, would we? I mean, there's the welcome party tonight, isn't there?'

'To hell with it,' Rose said. 'We can pay the fine. Or we come back, if you feel bad about it,' she added, seeing Clover's doubtful look. 'Oh, come on, Clovy. Don't let a pal down. I tell you I need cheering up. It's all right for you, with your pet Henry, but I'm beginning to feel like the little match girl.'

Clover wondered how Heinz would feel about it, but decided instantly in favour of Rose, who did look awfully glum.

'It'll do Heinz good to know I'm not his to command,' she said. Rose nodded.

'If he's as fond of you as I think he is, you'll need to be careful not to give him the wrong ideas.'

It was a bright, sunny day after a clear and freezing night, and the streets were full of skiers on their way to the slopes.

'They'll be going down like ninepins up there today,' Rose said. 'The trails will be like glass after last night. Pity the poor blood-waggon men lumbering up and down all day with stretcher-cases.'

As they drove away from Gries, Rose was growing more cheerful, and even Clover felt better for the change of scenery. 'I must say, though, nice though the weather is for sightseeing, we need a few good falls of snow. Some of the trails up there are getting thin, and with the peak season starting there'll be more people than ever wearing them down.'

They parked in the car park by the Hofgarten and set out in the bright winter sunshine to walk through the old quarter. They strolled along the arcaded streets and cobbled passages, lined with shops displaying beautiful leatherwork, embroidery and hand-carving, gold and silverwork, jewellery, and the sort of expensive, severely tailored clothes that the Germans loved to buy.

'It's like a kind of baroque Bond Street,' Clover said.

'At baroque-bottom prices,' Rose said. 'Just try translating that one into real money,' referring to the price-tag on a handbag. Clover did so and gulped.

'Are you sure you came here to spend money?' she asked Rose.

'Here, but not here. There's a boutique round the corner and across the road where I thought I might get a dress. Don't want to get caught short again, do I, if we get any more posh invitations?'

'You shouldn't let yourself be bullied,' Clover said. 'This is the age of equality.'

'Well, you know what that advertisement says – when was the last time a man told you you had a great pair of skis?'

'I think it's your poles he fancies,' Clover said.

They found the boutique which, with its traditional open racks of clothes and loud background music made a strange contrast to the hushed and select atmosphere of the rest of the shops. Rose, evidently feeling more at home, spent a long time going through the clothes and trying things on, until eventually she came up with a pretty imitation-crêpe dress in an attractive shade of lilac.

'Very fetching,' Clover said. 'If that doesn't fetch him, nothing will.'

'Oh hush,' Rose said. 'It's unlucky to talk about it.'

'You are a superstitious old thing. Where shall we go for

106

lunch? I'm hungry.'

'There's a lovely little coffee house I know down near the Ottoburg. It looks over the river. We can lunch there. I only discovered it the other Saturday when I came in to meet you. It's quite out of the way, and very quiet.'

It was so much out of the way that Rose couldn't find it, took two wrong turnings before remembering the narrow alley off a side road. She was triumphant at the feat of memory involved in bringing Clover safely to it, which made it all the more amusing for Clover when, hardly had they seated themselves, Val and George walked in. They stared in amazement, Rose turned red, and Clover choked over her coffee with laughter.

'Hullo-ullo-ullo,' Val said.

'What a sell!' Rose exclaimed indignantly. 'This is my very own special secret private place that I've just discovered for myself privately, and my friends, on our own, alone. And then you walk in. You are a pain, you two.'

'I could say the same, except that I'm too much of a gentleman,' Val said. 'But we'll go again, if you like.'

'No, no, stay now you're here,' Rose said hastily. 'I wouldn't turn you out into the snow.' George looked significantly over his shoulder at the bright sunshine outside and smiled.

'Such generosity. I should think the least we could do in that case is to buy you two ladies lunch, don't you think, Val?'

'Oh, indubitably,' Val said. 'If they'll have us.'

Clover, looking from face to face, saw how all four of them had brightened up because of this chance meeting. What fools we mortals are, she thought. We let such silly things govern us.

They had a very cheerful and frivolous lunch together, and Clover was surprised at how relaxed the two men were all of a sudden, joining in with Rose's best quality lunatic clowning without any regard to the dignity of seniority. She herself was rather quieter than usual, not from any lowness of spirits, but because she was savouring the occasion and the complementary personalities of Rose and Valentine and George. I shall remember this occasion, she told herself: it had that quality.

'Do you know what I'd like to do this afternoon?' Rose said suddenly when they were at the lingering stage of lunch. 'I'd love to go to the zoo. I haven't been to the zoo for – oh, ages and ages.'

There was a brief silence as they looked at each other, and then George suddenly smiled and said, 'Come on then. What are we waiting for?'

'We might as well be hung for kids as lambs,' Val said, jumping up.

'You're beginning to sound like me,' Rose said. Val put an arm round her shoulder and kissed the top of her head.

'What a nice idea. I can't think of anyone I'd sooner begin to sound like.'

They walked on ahead, and George and Clover exchanged an indulgent smile, feeling briefly like the parents of extremely talented children, before following them.

They drove to the Alpine Zoo in George's car, leaving Rose's in the car park to be collected later. Clouds were beginning to gather in the corners of the blue blanket of a sky, but the sunshine still held and it was almost as warm as spring until you stepped into the shade. The zoo was in the suburbs of the city, on the lower slopes of a mountain, and was beautifully laid out. The four of them wandered round it like children let out of school, telling each other anecdotes of past visits to other zoos and from there to childhood memories, telling jokes, and clowning, until it began to get dark, and they discovered a common desire for afternoon tea.

They found a café, and settled at a table, and looked at each other affectionately.

'There's nothing like a brisk limp down memory lane, is there?' Rose said. 'We've got a great future behind us. Hard to think we've only known each other a few days, isn't it?'

'Not George and me,' Val said in like vein. 'George and

I went to different schools together. We've known each other since we first met.'

George shook his head. 'I can't cope,' he said. 'I'm going to ignore you two and have an intellectual conversation with Clover.'

'What, me?' she gaped. Rose giggled.

'In future, stick to the past,' she warned him.

'I'd make you a present of my future,' Val countered, 'only I think I'm past it.'

'Talking of the future,' George said, 'we'd better keep an eye on the time. We've got to get back, you know.'

Val and Rose groaned in unison. 'Do you have to spoil it?' Rose said. He ignored them and looked round at the coffee house in which they were sitting.

'They must make a pretty good living in a place like this,' he said. 'I've often thought I'd like to go in for something like this. Not necessarily a coffee house, but perhaps a hotel or a bed-and-breakfast place, maybe with a restaurant attached. You could make a good thing out of it if you chose the right spot.'

'What spot?' Clover asked. Val answered for him.

'I can guess,' he said. 'A nice little exclusive ski-ing hotel at Aviemore, eh, George? Hame sweet hame, and rook the tourists, even as ye have been rooked also.'

'It's not a matter of rooking,' George said indignantly. 'You can charge what you like as long as people feel they're getting value for money. That's where the British generally go wrong.'

Clover listened with interest as the conversation developed from there. It was the first time she had seen anything of the ambition that Val had talked about, and while George was talking about his dream-enterprise, he sounded quite different, brisk and cheerful and energetic, without any of the defeat and sadness she had noticed in him at other times. Val alone noticed that she was quieter than usual, and discreetly he did not mention it but only looked at her speculatively from time to time. When she caught his eye upon her, she smiled reassuringly.

At half past four they started back, and at Val's

instigation he went back in Rose's car while Clover accompanied George. For whose benefit she could not be sure, but George seemed quite happy with the idea, and almost chattered as he drove her back to Gries. Clover had never seen him so cheerful, but he grew quieter as they drove down the Zell valley and drew nearer home. When they finally arrived at the village he drove on down the main road until he came to the apartment house where the seniors lived, and stopped outside it. He seemed to ponder a question for some time, and at last said, without looking at Clover, 'I wonder if you'd care to come in for a little while, and have a drink with me? We've time before dinner.'

'Thank you,' Clover said gravely, hiding her surprise out of tactfulness. 'I should like that.'

NINE

THE APARTMENT block was new and purpose-built, only three storeys high, but then no building was very tall in Gries. George's flat was on the top floor. When he opened the door it led into a tiny hallway with a parquet floor and pine-panelled walls and ceiling which was practically the norm in that part of the world but would have cost the professional middle classes of Chiswick a fortune. There were three closed doors. George indicated those to left and right.

'Bathroom, if you need it, and kitchen. And through here is the living room.' He opened the third door, the one straight ahead, and by the set of his shoulders as he led her in she knew he was proud of what she was about to see, which prepared her a little. He stepped aside, and the first thing to catch her eye was the window opposite, which took up almost the whole wall and looked out over the dark river and the promenade along its bank which was strung with lights like strings of pearls.

'How lovely!' she exclaimed and went towards it, noting out of the corner of her eye the pleased expression on George's face. 'It must be an absolutely fabulous view in daylight.'

'It is. You can see right across to the mountains opposite. It's almost a bit unreal, like those posters they stick up in frames in London cafés that are supposed to look like windows. But the colours, and the sense of space – it's awesome.'

'I'd love to see it sometime.'

'Of course,' he said, and he looked a bit embarrassed, so

111

Clover changed the subject slightly and looked round the rest of the room. She was surprised by it, though there was no real reason why she should have been. It was simply that she hadn't thought George would make any particular mark on the place where he lived, and yet this room was full of personal touches.

'This room is really lovely,' she said. 'I like your taste very much.'

'There really isn't any scope for the interior decorator in these panelled rooms,' George said, 'but the curtains and carpets and everything else that isn't built-in are mine.'

The room was oblong, with the great window on a long wall. The short wall to the left was dominated by an enormous dutch stove, well blackleaded, and with a fire door that could be opened so that the flames could be enjoyed. There were shelves built in to the alcoves to either side, and these were packed with books as solidly as only a reader would pack them – they hadn't the careful look of books that had been chosen as decoration. The floor was carpeted with a faded Turkish carpet which looked as if it really was old, and in front of the stove there was an enormous, thick, blonde fur rug.

The furniture was dark and leathery and the curtains brown and tweedy, which gave a solid, masculine air to the room, but this was mitigated by the one or two fine watercolours hanging on the walls and the delicate, beautiful curios that were scattered here and there on shelves and tables.

'The one thing I really miss,' George said, 'is flowers. I love to have flowers in the house, but here I have to make do with dried ones and preserved beech leaves and so on.' He gestured apologetically to a large terra-cotta urn in a corner which was filled with golden beech leaves and silver honesty and dried pink alpine roses.

'They're very pretty, anyway,' she said. 'You really have made the room lovely. Is this all you have?'

'Yes, apart from the bedroom through there, but that's very functional. Still, with the curtains open I've got the whole of the Zell valley in my living room, and you can't say fairer than that.' For a moment they stood staring out at the fairy-lit darkness. Then, he went forward and drew the curtains, and said, 'Now, what would you like to drink?'

'I'm very thirsty – could I possibly have coffee? Or is that too much trouble?'

'Nothing is too much trouble for you,' he said with what did not seem like gallantry. 'Would you like a drink as well?'

'Thank you – whisky then, if you have it.'

'Anything in it?'

'Of course not.'

He grinned. 'A woman after my own heart. Of course I wouldn't have refused you lemonade or ginger ale or whatever, but you'd have gone down in my estimation.'

Clover fanned herself. 'Phew, what a narrow escape.'

'Make yourself at home,' he said, 'while I go and get the coffee on. I won't be a minute.'

She wandered about examining things, and was standing looking at a painting when he came back with two tumblers of whisky.

'You like that?' he asked, handing her the glass.

'Very much,' she said. It was a grey-blue painting of an empty marsh and sky at dawn in winter. 'There's such stillness about it.'

'Yes, I know what you mean.' They stood side by side looking at it in silence for a moment, and then George turned his head and lifted his glass and said, 'Cheers.'

'Bung ho,' she said, clinking her glass against his; but she didn't at once drink, for he was closer than she had realised, and turning her head to him she found his face only inches away. Everything seemed to go very still for a moment, and in the intensified silence Clover thought he must hear her heart beating. She was suddenly terribly aware of him, as if she were feeling with his nerve-endings; but his face was too close for her to read his expression, and the moment passed, and they both drank, and George moved away and sat down on the sofa.

'Come and be comfortable,' he said, patting the seat

beside him. It was a long sofa, and when she sat down there was plenty of space between them. Her heart beats ought to be slowing down by now, but she gulped some more whisky and realised they weren't. Perhaps I'm being affected by the altitude, she thought, and smiled inwardly.

'It's a beautiful sofa,' she said for something to say. 'I've always liked a Chesterfield. Did you say that the furniture was yours?'

'Yes,' he said, shrugging. 'At first I lived in furnished digs, but after a while I thought, there's nothing to spend my money on, and any fool can be uncomfortable. So I made this place what I wanted.'

'But what will you do with it all when you go back to Britain?' Clover asked.

'Sell it. It would cost more than it's worth to ship it,' he said, and then realised, flicking a curious glance at her, that he had answered an assumption. 'But I don't know that I'll ever go back,' he added, not looking at her.

'Of course you will,' she said. 'What about this hotel in Aviemore?'

'Oh, that's just a pipe dream,' he said.

'Why only a pipe dream? There's nothing impossible about it,' Clover said. 'I thought it was really what you were going to do when you'd had enough of the Alps.'

He looked uncomfortable, and muttered, 'I've *had* enough of them.'

'Well then –' she said. He stood up and walked about the room.

'All of a sudden you're interested in my welfare,' he said irritably. 'Leave good works to the Red Cross – they're better at it.'

'I'm sorry,' Clover said, too surprised by his rudeness to be offended.

'I don't need taking care of,' he said.

'I'm sorry,' Clover said again, and he threw back his whisky.

'Do you want some more?' he said abruptly.

She shook her head, and he stalked out of the room and she heard him banging about in the kitchen. A few moments later he came back with the coffee things on a tray and a sheepish expression on his face. He put the tray down on the coffee table and then looked hesitantly at her. He almost had his cap off and his hands behind his back.

'Look, I'm sorry,' he said. 'I was very rude to you.'

'You were,' she agreed equably.

'I'm sorry – will you forgive me? I don't know what came over me.'

'I was more surprised than upset,' she said. 'I didn't know what I'd done.'

He sat down with a sigh and began to pour the coffee. 'Black? Sugar? And are you sure you wouldn't like some more whisky? Look, I've brought the bottle.' He topped up her glass and said, watching his hands as he poured, 'It wasn't anything you did. I was taking out on you an irritability that was nothing to do with you. It's a curious thing, but as soon as a person takes someone for granted the first use they make of it is to take things out on them. That's why husbands and wives quarrel so often, when really the person nearest you is the last one you should be unkind to.'

'Have you been married?' Clover asked, almost holding her breath for fear of interrupting his mood of confidence.

'Yes, I was married once,' he said abruptly, and then paused for so long she thought she had done it after all; but after a while he went on, 'It was a long time ago. I was very young. We both were – I suppose that's what went wrong. We were married for three years, and then she left me and went off with another man. It was just after the accident when I hurt my back. I've always thought it took a perverse kind of courage for her to leave me when I needed her most.' He looked up at Clover, but she thought he didn't really see her. 'It was a long time ago,' he said again. 'I've forgotten what she looked like. Is that shameful?'

'How old were you when you married?' she asked.

'Twenty-one,' he said. 'She was twenty.'

Before I met you, Clover thought, but she did not say it aloud. Instead she said, 'After all those years, it's natural to forget.'

His focus changed, and now he saw her.

'I shouldn't be boring you with this,' he said. She smiled.

'What a conventional thing to say, George,' she said, and saw his eyes flinch as she used his name. 'Why should you think I'd find anything about you boring?'

'You don't?' he said, and then changed it to, 'Don't you?' She shook her head, still with the small, closed-mouth smile. She thought she knew now what he was thinking about. 'But what about Heinz?' he said in what might have been an irrelevance, but wasn't.

'He's very fond of me,' Clover said casually. She had put down her cup while he was talking, and now as she saw him put down his, she said, 'You really have the most beautiful eyes. You shouldn't be allowed out with them.'

His smile now might have been the mirror-image of hers, and his face grew blurred as he leaned towards her, put his arms round her, looked quizzically down into her face for a moment, and then kissed her. She saw his eyes close before she closed her own, and felt his lips come down on hers with an impact that was like a short thick iron bolt right through the centre of her chest. Her arms went up and she held his face in her hands, feeling the softness of his cheeks which was so different from the child-like softness of Heinz's, and her heart lurched again. Good God, the separate part of her mind said in astonishment, you love him.

As she cupped his face in her hands, his arms went round her and pulled her in harder against him; her tongue came to meet his halfway and as desire arrived with a thump in her belly she felt it happen to him at the same moment. For a moment she abandoned herself to love, and then she felt him gradually draw back into himself and she knew he was not going to do anything about it. She was more disappointed than surprised. Men are so much less good at recognising what is happening to them, she thought. The kissing grew more shallow, and he broke the surface at last, and rested his head on her shoulder for a while, still holding her but unable at once to face her.

When finally he drew back he looked searchingly at her face as a person looks in through a window to see if there is anyone there. There were a couple of thousand questions in the expression of each of them, but since he put none of them into words, none of them got answered. He disengaged himself gently and cleared his throat with a nervous cough, and reached with an automatic, defensive gesture for his glass. It made her want to laugh, and to shake him, and to say, *Fool, I love you*; but you can't hurry them, she knew, and so she said nothing, and gradually the temperature in the room returned to normal.

'Well,' he said after a very long pause.

'Well,' she echoed, and reached for her coffee, and drank it thirstily. 'Could I have some more?' she asked. 'I really have got a raging thirst.'

'Of course,' he said, and she could hear how relieved he was that nothing irrevocable was going to be said. I'm a fool to myself, she thought, watching him pour with a hand that was not yet quite steady. 'And then I think you'd better be going if you aren't to miss your dinner. Welcome party tonight, don't forget, eight until ten.'

'I hadn't forgotten,' she said, and draining her cup, she stood up.

'I'll drive you back to the hotel,' George said, getting up too.

'I'd like the walk,' Clover said.

'I'll walk you back, then,' he said. She smiled.

'No, it's all right. Really. I'll be all right. Please don't bother.'

'If you're sure,' he said doubtfully.

'I'm sure.'

He accompanied her to the door. 'Thank you for a lovely day,' he said.

'I enjoyed it too,' she replied. She wanted him to kiss her again, but did not know what to do without appearing too forward.

'Um – tomorrow –' he began uncertainly.

'Is Sunday,' she said helpfully. He smiled in the way one

does at a distracting child, trying to think.

'In the afternoon, after lunch, I was thinking of ski-ing across to Janspitze. There's a rather nice little inn there, and it's an interesting trail, about five miles each way. Would you feel like doing that?'

'I'd love to,' she said. If he wasn't going to make the move, she'd have to. She reached up and put her mouth to his. 'Goodbye for now,' she said. For the fraction of a second she felt the response before it became just a polite farewell. She went down and out into the street and walked back to the hotel, two inches above the snow all the way.

'Of course, the problem is Heinz,' Clover said. She was sitting on the end of Rose's bed while the latter finished her make-up. They were already late for dinner, but Clover certainly didn't care, and Rose was always more interested in news than food.

'In what way is he a problem?' she asked. Her voice was distorted because she was pulling her face into an extra-ordinary shape in the effort to keep her eyelashes still for the mascara brush.

'Well, I don't imagine telling him will be easy,' Clover said.

'Aren't you being just the tiniest bit previous, heartface? I mean all the captain has done is give you a plonker on the phiz. You haven't even been invited to the dorm after lights out yet.'

'Yes, but I —' Clover hesitated.

'Yes, but you, what?' Rose said sternly. 'I hope you aren't going to tell me that you've fallen in love. It's the height of bad manners to fall in love with someone before they fall in love with you, old horse.'

'At that rate, no one ever would. They'd all be waiting for the other to begin.'

'Just testing, to see if you're still awake,' Rose said. She put down her mascara brush and turned round. 'Look, I believe in a bit of insurance. Why chuck Heinz away before you've actually signed the contract with George?

Love one and screw the other. What's the odds, as long as they're 'appy?'

'You're echoing my thoughts of a week ago – one man for one thing and one for the other,' Clover said.

'Well then.'

'I don't know. The thing is, I think George wouldn't like it. And if Heinz really is fond of me it will upset him. And I shall feel bad about it.'

Rose threw up her hands in exasperation. 'All I can suggest,' she said, 'is that you join a nunnery. That'll solve all your problems.'

'Lot of help you are. You'd better show me a bit more sympathy if you want my help with you and Val.'

'Who says I need help,' Rose said smugly. 'Listen, mate, the day you can tell me how to get on with Val, I'll wring your neck.'

'What happened in the car?'

'Not much. Enough, though. And of course I don't have your problem, because Kris and I are off, inasmuch as we were ever on. He's asked me to go out with him tomorrow afternoon, ski-ing to Janspitze.'

Clover grinned. 'Well well. I expect we'll see you there, then.'

Rose did a creditable double-take.

'What? Oh, I see, it's another foursome, is it? What's the matter with these two aged stiffs? Before you know it, it'll be a double wedding, and holding each other's hand in the bedroom afterwards. They're like a pair of kippers – two-faced and no guts.'

'Yes, and talking of that, we'd better kipper close eye on the time – it's nearly quarter past. We'll have missed the soup.'

'Hallelujah. One of these days I'm going to have a sharp word with Jock, about the food. I mean it's all very well serving up this foreign muck now and then, but what happened to good old egg and chips, and mince-tatties-an-peas?'

'Oh, don't,' Clover said. 'You're making my mouth water. Think of sausages and baked beans –'

'Steak and kidney pud –'

'– roast beef and yorkshire –'

'– but we'll go down there, and behold, it will be veal or chicken followed by ice cream. Lo! we travail in strange lands!' She stood up. 'Okay, I'm ready. Wop nosh detail fall in.'

'Never mind, tomorrow they can buy us a meal at Janspitze. A pity you can't wear your new dress for the occasion.'

'Isn't it. I shall have to abide, like Dan, in my breeches.'

'I need advance warning of your conversations,' Clover said, following her out.

'Don't worry – as someone once remarked to me last week, I talk mainly for my own pleasure.'

George made only a very brief appearance at the welcome party, and Val told Clover via Rose that he had had to go off and do other things down at the office. It made matters easier in one way, in that she could concentrate on Heinz, but in another way, concentrating on Heinz was not the best thing to be doing, for it only made him see her more firmly as half of a pair, of which he was the other half!

The welcome party was officially over at ten – that is to say, the lehrers were not obliged to stay for longer than that – but most of them did stay on. The party was held at the disco, which Ernst worked, throwing out between-records patter in a remarkable blend of English, German, Dutch and French, and it was not until he finally pulled out the plug at one o'clock that anyone thought of leaving. The Hot Max lehrers, except for Rose, and with the addition of Bruno's girlfriend, walked back to the annexe together. It was snowing heavily, and a wind was getting up.

'Good, we needed snow,' Heinz said, putting a protective arm round Clover. She did not like to shrug him off in front of the others, knowing he would find it hurtful to his pride, so she let it go, deciding that she would tell him in the privacy of his room. 'The trails were getting thin. Let us hope that this goes on all night.'

'But without the wind,' Clover suggested. 'That'll make ski-ing difficult.'

Bruno looked up and sniffed the air. 'The wind will die down,' he said confidently. Clover smiled to herself – Bruno always knew.

'Better than the BBC,' she murmured. They crowded into the lift together and fell out at the top, heading for their rooms without more than a brief good night. Clover, feeling apprehensive, followed Heinz into his room. As soon as she had closed the door he took her in his arms and tried to kiss her. She stiffened and tried to hold him back, and after a moment he let her go and stared at her, puzzled.

'What is it? What is wrong?' he asked.

'Heinz, I have to tell you something,' she said hesitantly. His wild eyes opened wider, making him look ferocious and dangerous.

'What? I do not like this beginning. You want to tell me something bad, I know.'

'Not bad. It's only that – well, I can't go to bed with you any more. I'm sorry.'

'Are you?'

'Yes.'

'Why? If you don't like me any more –'

'I do like you. I like you just as much as I always did,' she began, and he stepped towards her again.

'In that case,' he said, taking her in his arms. She turned her face away from him.

'No, Heinz. I like you, but –'

'There is someone else,' he finished for her. 'But who is this someone else?' He stared penetratingly at her face for a second and then said, 'Not this George? Clover, you are mad! He will not love you. He does not want young girls. He will give you nothing. You are fool if you think he wants you.'

Clover stared helplessly. 'That's my business.'

'Mine too, if he takes you from me.'

'I don't belong to you, Heinz. You have to realise that,

121

if you don't understand anything else. I belong to me and no one else.'

'But you are my lover. And I love you, Clover. I love you, and I am young man, I can make you happy. He does not want you, that old man.'

She had to laugh. 'He isn't an old man, don't be silly.'

Heinz, following up the advantage he thought her laughter had given him, began kissing her neck and running his hands over her shoulders and down her sides, and Clover shuddered – she couldn't help it.

'You see,' Heinz murmured, 'you see you still want me. You know it. We are so good together, Clover, we make such good love. Come, come to bed, you will forget him at once.' His hands were sliding up inside her jumper, and though she pushed at him it was weakly, ineffectually. The sweet smell of him, the warmth of his body, his animal beauty – they were here and George was not. Was Rose right, was Heinz right? Was she foolish to turn this away for a mere outside chance? Physically, she wanted Heinz, and if he wanted her, and it would give them both pleasure, where was the harm? Time enough to be making vows of chastity to George when he showed that he wanted them, that he was going to make them in return.

Heinz murmured again. 'Lovely, lovely one. Come, let us go to bed.' His lips travelled up from the hollow of her shoulder, slid across her face to her mouth. His hands were on her breasts, and with a sigh of resignation she stopped pushing him away and folded her arms round his slender body and gave him her mouth. The taste of him was familiar and lovely, the touch of him was exciting. All she had to do was let go.

TEN

For once they slept late, and when they did wake, Heinz would not let Clover get up, but prepared coffee for her and brought it to her in bed, and then got back in with her and made love until lunch-time, dozing in between whiles. It was a pleasant way to spend Sunday morning; the only thing missing was the *Observer* and the English breakfast and the sound of lawnmowers from outside. Outside instead was snow which fell lightly and steadily until mid-morning, after which the skies began to clear, and by half past twelve the sun was shining.

Clover got up then, ready to head for the bathroom, when Heinz began to talk about lunch. She didn't want to tell him at that point about George and the run to Janspitze, so she told him firmly that she was lunching with Rose and spending the afternoon with her, which was true, if not the whole truth.

'I can come too,' Heinz complained. 'Rose is my friend also.'

'You can't,' Clover said, trying not to feel matronly. 'We want to have girl-talk. We want to be private.'

He complained again and she began to get cross, though aware that part of her crossness was guilt.

'Look, Heinz, I can't spend every waking minute with you. I don't want to. I want some time on my own too.'

'But you will not be on your own. You will be with Rose. And if you can be with Rose, why can you not be with me?'

'It isn't the same,' she said helplessly. 'Being with Rose is like being on my own. Anyway. I'm not having lunch

123

with you and that's all there is to it. I'm sorry.'

'I think you are not sorry,' he said, throwing himself over in bed so that his back was to her. Clover took the opportunity and went out, closing the door softly behind her. She drew a deep breath on the other side. It was very difficult being the one who was more loved than loving. She had thought it would be harder the other way about but she was not sure now.

She and Rose went up to the lodge for lunch, which was where they were to meet the men, but the moment they went out into the sunshine, on their way up the mountain Clover felt something significant must happen.

'I shall have to do something about Heinz,' she said. 'It seems the more I put him off the stronger he becomes.'

'That's men all over,' Rose said. 'They're perverse buggers, every one. They'll never love where they're loved or do what they're supposed to do. God, the snow looks good today. I could eat it!'

'I know what you mean,' Clover said. 'It looks as exciting and inviting as syllabub or sorbet. And the colour of the sky! If you saw it on a postcard you'd think it had been faked with a blue filter.'

The sky was so dark a blue it was almost gentian, and the snow was glittering and blue enough to make your eyes ache, so that it was a positive relief to look at the dark line of the trees or the deep gold of the walls of the lodge. The sun was hot, too, and the two girls took their lunch on the terrace with their jackets off and their sleeves rolled up. They were only halfway through when the two men arrived.

They exchanged greetings, and Clover felt absurdly shy of George until she saw that he too was shy, and that gave her confidence. Really, she thought, we're two grown adults; if one of us doesn't keep the ball rolling we'll get nowhere.

George waved a key at her and said, 'If you wouldn't mind coming with me to the store, I think you ought to try a long pair of skis for this afternoon. The trails are going to be quite fast and smooth, and you'll find it less tiring.'

Clover got up at once, but Val nudged her and said, 'You fall for his soft talk every time, don't you? He only wants to get you in a dark place alone, you know.'

'Well, what makes you think I don't want to be got in a dark place alone,' Clover countered. George looked slightly put out, but Val grinned and nodded.

'Quite right – I hadn't thought of that. Off you go children, with my blessing. Only don't forget we ought to be on the way by two to make the most of the daylight hours.'

George had recovered himself sufficiently to look at his watch and say, 'All right, if we haven't reappeared by five to two you can send a search party.'

'And a stretcher,' Val added. 'It's only twenty past one now.'

After all the chai-acking, Clover expected George to be even more nervous than before, but when he had led them into the store and put on the light, he closed the door and turned to her with a small smile.

'He isn't entirely wrong, of course,' he said.

'I'm glad of that,' Clover said. 'I would have been worried if I thought I was that unattractive.'

'Unattractive? My God!' George said, licking his lips nervously. 'It's only that I find you too damned attractive. Once started I'm afraid I'd never be able to leave off.'

Clover met his eyes inexorably, and with an indrawn breath that sounded like exasperated surrender, he stepped forward and put his hands on her shoulders. He looked questioningly into her face, and said, 'Look, I –'

'What?' she murmured. He gave the ghost of a shrug, and kissed her. It was a light, tentative kiss on both cheeks, but quickly took on another character as they set each other alight, and after a few moments it was Clover who broke away, aware that this was not the time nor the place for explorations of that sort. 'Later, you fool, later,' she said, making light of it. He drew back quickly.

'You're right. To business. I really didn't mean – I mean I didn't come here to –'

'It's all right. I wish you could realise that you don't

have to keep apologising to me,' Clover said. For some reason, he seemed to take this wrongly.

He cooled fractionally, and said, 'No, I suppose I don't. Let's look at these skis.'

Because she did not know what was in his mind, she could not hunt up the possible misunderstanding, and so with a shrug she became business-like too, trusting that two sane, intelligent adults couldn't remain at odds with each other except by wanting to. They chose her some skis, and went out again into the sunshine. George seemed slightly ill at ease, and Clover hoped the other two wouldn't indulge their wit at his expense when they rejoined them, but fortunately Val and Rose were playing a verbal game of Dismember the Guests, and George and Clover were able to sit down again without comment.

They set off at ten to two, and took the sesselbahn up to Rosenhof to begin with, and started there by ski-ing along the almost flat ridge that ran along the crest of the Rosenberg. Clover felt tremendously exhilarated. It was the first long ski she had embarked on for years, and it made a great difference to feel that you were actually going somewhere, instead of going up and down the same stretch of mountainside over and over again. It was more interesting, too, to be ski-ing across country instead of on groomed and much-travelled trails. As they went they left tracks in unmarked snow. Our own personalised marks, she thought to herself.

Val led the way, and Rose came after him, then Clover and George last, but when they came to the first short downhill run they spread out and took their own paths, which again is part of the fun of off-piste ski-ing. The snow was in perfect condition, and Clover felt tremendously happy. They rounded another shoulder and came to the first long fast run of the day, and in a matter of moments they were racing each other like horses let loose on a hillside. Clover, being a skater, found the inner-ski turn the easiest and most natural to use on a downhill run, and with a short radius it is a very fast turn too, so she quickly gained on and passed Rose, and zigged-zagged lightly down the fall-line and almost caught Val on the schuss.

When they came to a levelling-out Val signalled a stop, and in a moment they were gathered together, leaning on their poles, pushing up their goggles and panting, grinning at each other like excited dogs.

'You're fast,' Rose said to Clover. 'You went past me like a speed-skater.'

'I loved watching you Charlestoning down in front of me,' George said. 'Of course, a couple of years ago what you were doing would be considered very incorrect, ski-ing on your inside ski. In fact, I don't think it could have been me that taught you that particular turn.'

'It wasn't,' Clover said with a sheepish grin. 'You were always a great stylist above all things. I learnt it in Switzerland, but it's the most comfortable for me, I find.'

'See what happens,' George said to Val. 'Other instructors corrupting my pupils.'

'Good for her balance,' Val said. 'Look, you can see the village we're heading for – there, in the fold of the hill down there.'

'Oh, yes. It doesn't look very far,' Rose said.

'Distances are deceptive,' Val said. 'Remember that, if you ever go out on your own, you two girls.'

'Yes, Dad.'

'None of that, cheek-box,' Val said sternly. 'You won't be able to see the village once we leave this shoulder. We go down there, into that gully, and then I'm afraid we have a climb, but only a short one up to that point there, and then it's downhill all the way.'

'How do we get back?' Clover asked.

'I could almost see your logical mind working round to that one,' Val said. 'We langlauf back, along the line of the road, but a little higher up. Then when we get nearer home, if you like we can take a lift up and get a downhill for the last mile or so.'

'Depending on how tired you are,' George added. Clover and Rose exchanged a glance.

'They think we aren't fit,' Rose observed. 'I wonder

what they think we do all day?'

'We wonder all right, but we're too polite to ask,' Val said. 'Come on, my bairns, let's go.'

It was a lovely day, and after that first break any awkwardness between them was gone. They spent almost an hour at the inn in the village of their destination, and found themselves chatting without any restraint like old friends. It was a return to the happiness of the previous day. Clover noticed the increased intimacy between Rose and Val, often wandering off into conversation together, leaving Clover and George verbally alone. Clover was glad of it. She knew now, more or less, what her feelings towards him were; she wanted him to have the opportunity of discovering his feelings for her. They seemed increasingly warm. By the time they were ready to leave again, he had been holding her hand under the table for some time, and when they stood up and Val walked off with his arm round Rose, there seemed no point in his being secretive about it any more. He exchanged a smile with Clover, and then put his arm round her.

Clover relaxed. It would be all right, she felt. He was only uncertain of himself through long disuse of that particular social faculty. Tonight, she thought, tonight it ought to be all right. There was the lehrers' meeting, of course, at which he would preside, and that might set him back a step or two, but she hoped that it would be only a temporary relapse. She watched him covertly all the way home, admiring all over again the neat and graceful actions of his body, the gravity of his face when he concentrated, the wonderful illumination of his smile when he turned to her in pleasure and exhilaration. There was such a deep reserve of sadness in him, that it seemed to her miraculous that she could be the cause of its lifting, however temporarily. If he would love her, perhaps the sadness would eventually be drained away.

When they got near to the village they stopped to discuss whether or not to do the last downhill run, and while Val was all for getting back for hot baths and food, the others were still keen to try it, so he gave in gracefully and they took the lift to the top. There was a short and difficult black run, and then an easy traverse over on to their own Rosenberg and the long run down past the lodge and crossing under the cables. They had dismounted from the sessellift and were standing together near the beginning of the run preparing to set off when Clover heard her name called, and turned with a sinking of heart to see Heinz coming towards her.

'But what are you doing here?' he asked, his face lighting up as he poled up to her. 'If I had known you would be here we could have gone together. Have you been up here all afternoon?'

He had not seen George, who was kneeling down checking his bindings, but as George straightened up, Heinz's eyes met his, and they stared at each other with the hostility of two cats. Heinz's eyes went to Clover's face, and his expression darkened.

'You said you would be with Rose,' he said angrily.

'So I am,' Clover said with a gesture.

'You lied to me, you said you were lunching with Rose, but here I see you have been all day with him. Why did you lie to me? Why?'

Clover was irritated by his melodramatic outburst. Really, she thought, I can't have this.

'I didn't lie to you. What I do with my time is my affair. Behave yourself, Heinz. You have no right to speak to me like that.'

'Have I not?' He stared from Clover to George, whose face was inexpressive as granite. 'Is it to be him, now, then? And not me any more? You are cruel, a cruel woman. You know that I love you. Please, Clover –'

The plea was unspecific, but perfectly comprehensible, too comprehensible to all four of the people trying, in embarrassment, to avoid his gaze.

'I didn't ask you to love me,' Clover said in desperation. 'I won't be bullied, Heinz. You must leave me alone.'

A moment longer he stared, his face red with suppressed

129

emotions, and then he cried out, 'I see. Yes, I must leave you alone. I shall do – and then you may be sorry!'

With that he jerked his goggles down over his face, and turned, took the two steps to the head of the run and flung himself over the start with the kind of jump ski-jumpers use to start their run-up. The four of them watched him go and exchanged glances.

'What did he mean by that?' Clover said nervously.

'Nothing, I should think,' Val said, but he didn't sound certain. Rose shrugged.

'He can look after himself. He's a good skier – one of the best.'

'But he's upset,' Clover said.

'We'd better follow him,' Val decided, pulling his goggles down. Clover glanced again at George. Only he had said nothing, and his face was grim. She could not guess what he was thinking, but he followed them anyway, and they set off down the run, Val in the lead and Clover close behind him, so close that his snow-spray was hitting her face.

'There he is,' Val shouted. Heinz was a good way ahead, and going very fast.

'Too fast,' Clover shouted back.

'He's good,' Val offered her his own comfort, but he increased speed anyway. He'll be all right, Clover told herself firmly. He's a better skier than any of us. He had schussed almost the whole of the first drop, which they had to traverse, and his speed had built up rapidly on the fast snow. He made a turn at the first shoulder of the hill, and Val gave a grunt at the sight of it.

'Too bloody fast,' he muttered. They watched the flying figure, smaller now, heading for the second shoulder, where the terrain fell away in a short steep precipice. The run made its second turn there, this time to the left. They saw Heinz throw himself into the turn, shoulder and hip, but at the same moment Val yelled, 'He's too close to the edge! The bloody fool –!'

The snow had built out into a ledge over the drop, and Heinz's speed was too great to make the turn sharply enough on the narrow neck of the trail. Almost in slow motion they saw the great chunk of snow break off, crumbling like fresh cake along the crack and distintegrating into flying white powder as it fell, taking the small starfish shape of the skier with it. In the clear air they heard him cry out, a short, cut-off cry that reached them fractionally before the rumble of the snow-slip.

They increased their speed, though what good they imagined they could do, no one knew. Only George kept his head, braking and making a U-turn with his momentum, shouting over his shoulder, 'I'll get help.'

Clover saw Val's white face turn briefly back in acknowledgement and one stick go up to signal he had heard. Her brain was numb. She raced on behind Val with no thought in her head but to get there. Beyond that she was mercifully blank.

By the time they reached the site of the fall, others coming from further down the mountain were already there and digging. Val took control as soon as he arrived, and the other skiers, mainly guests, were obviously relieved at his role of authority. He was only lightly covered, and within a minute Val was brushing the snow from Heinz's mouth and nose while directing Clover, curtly, to remove his skis.

'Don't move his legs, though,' he added. 'I think they're broken.' Clover found her hands trembling, and she controlled them only with an effort.

'Is he alive?' she managed to ask. Val was examining him with quick light hands.

'He's still alive. I don't know how badly hurt he is.' He glanced upwards. 'Not so much of a fall, thirty feet maybe. Depends how he landed.'

Heinz remained unconscious. His body was twisted at the waist, and after a careful examination Val concluded that he might have damaged his back or pelvis. In that case, there was nothing he dared do to ease Heinz's position, other than loosen the clothes at his neck and cover him with all the offered jackets.

'We must just wait until the blood-waggon arrives,' Val

said. His face was white and strained, but he sounded blessedly calm, and Clover found herself instinctively huddling nearer to him for comfort. Rose squatted beside her and put her arms round her. They had both given their jackets up, and could pretend it was for warmth. Clover looked at the soft shadow of the boy's eyelashes on his cold cheek, and wondered what would come of it all. Val said it wasn't much of a fall, which presumably meant he had known worse, but to her it looked terrible, and she knew that though the snow looked soft and billowy, it was not at all soft to fall on.

The wait seemed interminable, though it could not have been more than ten minutes or so, before the ambulance sled arrived and responsibility was taken from them. Heinz came to briefly when they moved him, and groaned, and vomited, but he relapsed into unconsciousness again when they lifted him on to the sled and strapped him immobile. They set off down the mountain, and Rose, Clover and Val replaced their skis and followed.

George had made good use of the time, and he and an ambulance were waiting at the bottom of the run. Still stony-faced, he said, 'Someone must go with him.'

'I'll go,' Val said. 'You've got the meeting to take.'

'All right. You'd better go too,' he added to Clover. She looked surprised. 'He'll want you there when he wakes up, and you'll only worry if you're not on the spot. Go on, they're ready now. Rose and I'll take your skis.'

There was no time to argue. Val scrambled up into the ambulance and held out a hand to Clover. She climbed in and sat down beside him. The last she saw of George before they slammed the doors shut behind her was his mask-like face watching her go.

The short journey to the hospital was the beginning of a strange dream, not really a nightmare because she found herself unable yet to feel very much. George had been right about one thing – Heinz recovered consciousness again in the ambulance and called out at once for Clover. She went to him and took his hand, but he looked at her unrecognisingly from under his eyelids and drifted off again. It might be very romantic in a book, she thought, but in real life it's an unwelcome responsibility.

At the hospital, they whisked him away on a wheeled trolley, and Val had to answer questions while the receiving nurse filled in a form. Then there was nothing to do but wait. They sat in a waiting room, and from time to time fetched or were brought cups of coffee. The main difference, Clover found herself thinking, between this and an English hospital was that it was coffee and not tea.

When finally they were called to speak to the doctor, he spoke in rapid German which Clover was by now too fuddled and weary to understand. She looked helplessly at Val, and he translated for her when the doctor had finished.

'He'll be all right,' he said. 'He's concussed and shocked, but he'll recover.'

That did not accord with the doctor's expression.

'And what else?' she said. Val gave a little gesture as if he would hold her hand, but didn't.

'He's got a broken pelvis,' he said. 'It's going to be a long job.'

Clover stared at him, and felt herself disintegrating. Her lips trembled, and the trembling spread downwards rapidly. Val took hold of her by the elbows.

'Bear up,' he said. 'This isn't the place to faint. That's a good girl, hold on to me.'

She nodded, and then managed to say, 'Can we see him?' The doctor answered in English.

'He is sedated, but you can go and see him for a moment. He will not wake again tonight, so there is no reason for you to stay.'

Funny, she thought, as they followed him down the corridor, the way all hospitals resent outsiders and don't want them cluttering up their hallowed precincts. In the room, they looked briefly at Heinz. Heavily asleep, his hair looked very dark against the white sheets, and he looked very young. Had she not known, she would have thought him only sixteen or seventeen. She began to cry, but silently, and Val took her arm again and took her

133

away.

Outside she was startled to find it dark, having forgotten the length of time they been waiting. She looked at Val helplessly, wondering what to do next.

'Come on,' he said, 'we both need a stiff drink. And something to eat. You're hungry.'

'Am I?'

'Yes. How do I know? Because I am. I know this place – there's a good inn along here.'

'I couldn't eat anything. I feel sick.'

'You'll eat. Come, trust me.'

'I do,' she said. He took her to the inn and ordered food, and got them both a large whisky while they were waiting, and the nausea retreated before the warmth of the spirit. They sat at the table, waiting for the food, and Clover felt utterly worn out.

'One thing, we'll miss the lehrers' meeting,' Val said. She couldn't raise so much as the twitch of the tail of a smile. 'Listen,' he said, reaching for her hand to make sure of her attention, 'you know that it isn't your fault in any way, don't you?'

'Yes,' Clover said dully, 'I know that.' He nodded and let her hand go, and he seemed at last to relax from his effort of keeping everyone's spirits intact. Suddenly, he looked ten years older.

'Poor little bugger,' he said. 'It'll be a long time before he skis again.'

ELEVEN

THE FEELING of being inside a dream did not fade. At first
there was an atmosphere of hush and distress over all the
lehrers, as they heard the news and thought of poor Heinz
suffering the fate they all dreaded for themselves; but it is
impossible to feel sympathy at that pitch for very long, and
soon their lives returned to normal. Even Rose and Val,
though not lacking in very sincere pity for the young man,
had far more to be happy about in each other than to be
sad about in the memory of the accident.

Only Clover and George seemed to go on suffering. On
the surface George's life returned to normal and the other
lehrers would never have noticed any difference. But those
who had grown closer to him could see that he was more
withdrawn and reserved even than before; that he never
appeared outside of working hours except on business;
that he no longer joined in even those few group activities
he had been seen at before. He had always appeared dour
but now he never smiled, though, paradoxically, he spoke
more gently to everyone, even when he had to reprimand
someone.

Clover was not in a position to notice this change at
first, because for the first two weeks she was only taking
classes in the mornings, while the afternoons saw her
driving, in Rose's car, to the hospital to sit with Heinz. On
his first waking he had asked for her, and he now clung to
her so fiercely that, while she was worried about its long-
term effect, she did not dare in the short term miss an
afternoon visit.

It was she who sat with him through the storms of tears

135

and the despair that first week when he had to be told that it would be months before he would ski again, and that in all likelihood he would never be completely fit again. He clung to Clover not as a lover but as a son, and she often wondered what his home life had been like, and where his parents were now. She felt that there was no great individual choice about her presence with him, but that he had decided early on what to cling to and was doing it with nothing more than consistency. She had no one to tell this to. Her life was becoming as isolated as George's.

After the first shock, Heinz became calmer, at least on the surface, and Clover's job then was simply to sit with him while he held her hand and talked. In this way bit by bit she heard all his story. His mother had left his father when he was quite small and had run off with a rich American who had been stationed in Germany after the war as an airman. He had stayed with his father until he died, and he had then been sent to school, staying with his mother and her husband during holidays. It was she who had had him taught to ski, and bit by bit ski-ing had taken the place in his life of mother, father, family and even God.

That was why he had become a nomadic lehrer – he had no home other than with his mother, and she made it clear that she did not welcome too frequent an intrusion from him. Clover wondered vaguely whether she physically resembled his mother, or whether there was some other trait in her that he saw as desirable in a mother-figure. She could not blame herself for the accident, but she wished she had never been involved with him at all, so that she would not have to sit here and remember.

She watched him as the second week turned into the third. Pain and pain-killing drugs normally age a person, but in Heinz's case the lethargy of his condition made him look younger, and his relaxed white face upon the pillow was like that of a young boy. From the third week she resumed full teaching hours, and came to visit him in the evenings. She fetched things for him, wrote letters for him, read to him, listened endlessly while he talked, and finally

136

drove back to Gries feeling exhausted, to bathe and fall into bed where she slept heavily and dreamlessly. Her mind seemed to come alive only during the short drive to and from the hospital, and then it was that, rousing from the strange torpor of this dream-like state, she regretted bitterly Heinz's smooth golden body, remembered in inexorable detail their last night together, wondered about his future, and longed for the comfort of talking to George. But George she had barely seen since the accident. She saw him sometimes at a distance while she was teaching or while she was collecting a class. Since the evenings were taken up with Heinz, she was excused the meetings and parties, and if he was anywhere around on other evenings, she was not to know.

She had scarcely spoken two words to Rose, either, for the same reason. She didn't even see Rose at breakfast now, for Rose was sleeping with Val at his apartment and breakfasted with him, and since Clover normally went straight to the hospital without dining first she did not see her in the evenings either. It all added to her sense of isolation. When the third week turned into the fourth, Clover began to feel that the time had come to start weaning Heinz off her. It was now December, Christmas was approaching. Surely it might be possible to fly Heinz home to his mother for Christmas? If she was as rich as his stories suggested, she ought to be able to arrange it.

But when she tentatively brought it up, his face grew sullen.

'My mother does not want me. It is not ''home'' as you call it. To go to her would not be to go home. Home is Gries now. But in any case, I could not leave the hospital yet. You know that I cannot be moved.'

She let it pass for the moment, but the next day she tried again, this time mentioning casually that she would not be able to visit him the next evening.

'Why not?' he demanded at once. She shrugged.

'I have something else to do. I have a life of my own to lead, you know.'

'But *what* do you have to do?' he insisted. 'Surely you

could do it in the daytime. It cannot be more important than coming here. What am I to do if you do not visit me?'

'Heinz, you can't depend on me for ever,' she said gently. He grabbed her hand.

'Why not?'

'Well, because I won't always be here. I shall be leaving at the end of the season anyway, and I can't spend every night between now and then visiting you.' She saw his face twist in a mixture of anger and panic and went on hastily, 'You won't be alone. The others will come and visit you. In fact I'm sure they'd have come before now if I'd asked them, only I expect they think you're too ill to be visited. But I'll ask some of them to come in tomorrow. I'm sure Ernst –'

'No!' he said, so loudly that a nurse passing the door of the room glanced in surprised. He was gripping her hand more and more tightly. 'I don't want Ernst. I don't want any of the others. I only want you. If they come I won't see them. You can tell them that. I will only see you.'

'Heinz, don't be silly. And please let go of my hand – you're hurting me.'

He did not, he only held her more tightly. 'You can't desert me,' he cried.

'Don't talk like that,' she said, trying not to sound angry. 'Desert you – what are you talking about? I'm not your mother.'

'No, you are my love,' he said.

'I'm not your love.'

'You were my lover.'

'Yes, I was. We were friends, that's all.'

'A friend is not all. And a friend does not desert a friend when he needs her.'

'Look, Heinz, we were friends, lovers if you like, but that was nothing out of the ordinary. You had lots of other girls, lots of the guests – I know, the others told me – and you don't expect them to spend their lives visiting you in hospital.'

'It was different with them. I did not love them. I love you.'

'I didn't ask you to love me,' Clover said helplessly, but he began to cry, letting go of her hand and placing his own over his face.

'You are so cruel,' he wept, and real tears trickled out between his fingers. 'You do not care if I live or die.'

Massaging the blood back into her hand, Clover stared at him in despair. You're right, she thought, ultimately I don't care. But I can't tell you that. Perhaps it would have been better if she could, but she could not be so blatantly cruel.

'Don't cry, Heinz, please. You know I'm fond of you –'

He broke off his sobbing abruptly and flung his hands down, staring at her in hope.

'You are fond of me! I knew it all along. Oh, Clover, don't talk about leaving me.'

This is like something out of a 1940's film, she thought, the dream-like sensation returning full strength. It was partly, of course, because they did not speak the same language, and in translation many things gain weight and importance.

Heinz held out his hand to her, and said more sensibly, 'You cannot leave me now, when I need you so much. You cannot be so cruel.'

Can't I? Clover wondered, but she gave him her hand all the same. It was not good for him to be upset.

'We won't talk about it now,' she said at last. He relaxed, happy enough with that. To the invalid all moments are present; he was content with a present victory. They talked of other things until it was time to go, but when she stood up he said, 'I will see you at the same time tomorrow.'

'No,' she said. 'I told you I couldn't come. Shall I ask Ernst to come in? Or Bruno?'

'No!' he shouted. 'I won't see them. I will only see you!'

She shrugged and walked to the door. 'As you please,' she said.

Seeing she would not relent, he waited until she was turning out of sight and then called, 'But you will come the next day?'

She heard the anxiety and latent panic in his voice. Little by little, she thought. That's the only way it can be done.

'Yes, I'll see you the next day,' she said.

When she arrived back in Gries it was ten o'clock, and she was hungry, tired and depressed, but also curiously restless. She could have gone straight to the Hot Max and eaten, bathed, and gone to bed, but she felt the need of contact with someone else. The isolation seemed to be threatening to build up into an impenetrable wall around her. For instance, though she had won a night off from Heinz tomorrow, she had no idea what she would do with it: the very idea of it made her feel lost. She drove past the hotel turn off, not really knowing where she was heading, until she found herself in the Bahnhofstrasse, and heading towards the apartment building. Then she knew what she wanted – she wanted to see George.

He might not be home, of course, in which case she did not know what she would do; but she parked the car anyway and went up in the lift, leaning against the door and almost falling out when it opened at the top. She leaned against the wall while she rang George's bell. She felt too tired to hold herself upright.

The door opened, and he looked at her without surprise, as if he had expected her to call.

'Come in,' he said. 'You look dead beat.'

'I feel it,' she said. She walked through to the living room and sat down on the sofa, leaned back and closed her eyes. After a moment, knowing he was standing looking at her, she forced them open again, and caught the tail end of an expression he did not mean her to see that she could not quite fathom – something watchful and curious. 'I'm sorry,' she said. He made a vague gesture of dismissal with his hand.

'What do you need?' he asked. 'Have you eaten yet?' She shook her head. 'You look as if you haven't been eating properly for some time. I'll get you something to eat. And some coffee.'

'Thanks,' she said, gratefully.

'Do you want a drink too?' he asked, being thorough. She nodded again. 'Scotch?' And again. Suddenly he smiled, albeit a short, strained smile. 'Rest,' he said. 'I'll see to everything.'

'God,' she murmured, 'if you could know how I've longed to hear someone say that.' She closed her eyes and lay back again.

'I know,' he said, and she followed the sound of his footsteps as he fetched a glass and the Scotch bottle. 'Don't you think I've felt like that at times? Everyone feels it sometimes.'

'I should think especially you,' she said. 'You have so much carrying to do.'

'Here.' She opened her eyes and took the glass from him. He had poured himself one, and watching her carefully he raised it and said, 'Cheers.'

'Cheers.'

He left her then without another word and went into the kitchen, shutting the door after him, and Clover was content just to lie back and sip her drink and wait. Before long he came back with coffee.

'Food will be a little while,' he said. 'Do you want something to keep you going?'

'I have it,' she said, and gestured with her glass, though it was not what she meant. As if he knew that, he sat down on the edge of the sofa and looked at her with a troubled expression. 'Talk to me,' she said. 'Or do you have to rush out to the kitchen?'

'It will cook itself for a while,' he said.

'You look tired too,' she said. 'I'll bet you haven't eaten tonight either.'

'No. Perhaps I knew you were coming.'

'Did you?'

'No.' She smiled, but he did not respond. 'Perhaps I hoped you were coming. How is the boy?'

'His condition is said to be comfortable,' she said dryly. 'It's his mind I'm worried about. George, is there any chance we could get him sent home to his mother?'

141

'I didn't know he had one.'

'Of sorts,' Clover said, and told him the story, a résumé of what Heinz had told her.

'It doesn't sound as if she'd be much use to him,' George said when she had finished. 'Are you sure he wants to go?'

'No. Quite the reverse. He doesn't want to go.'

'Then why do you want to be rid of him?'

'Because,' Clover said grimly, 'he doesn't want to go.'

'Oh?' George questioned, and his assumed neutrality of tone did not hide the disapproval underneath. She sighed.

'It isn't because I grudge the time or anything, but he's clinging to me like a lifebelt, and the longer he hangs on the harder it's going to be to prise his fingers loose. He can't use me as a prop all his life.'

'I'm not sure I understand,' George said, still carefully.

'He says he's in love with me, begs me to stay, calls me cruel when I told him I'd send someone else to visit him tomorrow. He gets hysterical at the idea of my not coming in. I don't think it's good for him.'

'But if he's in love with you – ?'

Clover held out her glass before replying, and George filled it absently.

'I don't think he is,' she said.

'But he thinks he is.'

'I suppose so.'

'But you aren't in love with him?'

'Of course not. There was never any question of it before – before the accident.'

George raised an eyebrow. 'But I thought you were –'

'We slept together. That's all.'

'All?'

Clover jerked her head angrily. 'Oh don't say "all" in that superior voice. For God's sake, you don't have to be in love with someone to have sex with them. You aren't going to tell me you swore undying love to every girl you ever took to bed, are you?'

He had the grace to look a little ashamed. 'I'm sorry. It

142

just goes against the grain to hear a woman say it, that's all.'

Clover gave an unwilling grin. 'I suppose you have your childhood teaching to overcome in this age of equality. But so long as you do try to overcome it –'

'Now and then,' he said. He looked at her with a question in his face that he wasn't going to ask.

She tried to guess what it was, and said, 'Of course it's preferable if one is in love with the person, but that's the ideal state. One aims at it but doesn't always achieve it.'

She had guessed right, it seemed. He nodded and reverted to Heinz.

'All the same, it seems – yes, cruel, I suppose, to desert the poor boy when his life is in ruins. When he's lost the only thing –'

'Oh come on, George,' she interrupted him. 'Don't over dramatise. You're as bad as he is. Point one, he will recover. He will ski again –'

'– perhaps.'

'– certainly. He won't be a hundred per cent fit, but what the hell?'

'It's easy enough for you to say that. You don't know what it's like to give up the one thing you're good at.'

'Maybe I don't, but it isn't that important. After all, it couldn't have lasted for very long anyway. You're only in top class competitions for a few years and then you're too old. How many times have I heard you and Val and the others say that sport – any sport, but this one in particular – is a dead end? Maybe it's a good thing that this happened to him, we don't know. Maybe it will get him to change his life while he's still young. There must be a thousand other things he could do. Already he uses ski-ing as a prop, and that's a situation which could only get worse for him as he got older.'

George still looked unconvinced. She drained her glass and held it out again, and he filled it without speaking.

'In any case,' she said, 'I'm not going to be blackmailed by him – or by anyone else. Of course I'm sorry he's hurt, but I'm not going to sacrifice my life for him.'

'Blackmail,' he said musingly. 'And sacrifice?'

'What else would you call it?' She looked at his face, and again sought and tried to answer the questions he was not putting. 'If I loved him it might be different, I don't know. If I loved him it might not seem like a sacrifice. But I don't, and I never did. I'm very fond of him, I feel affectionate towards him, but that's all.'

George nodded, and then got up and went into the kitchen, leaving Clover alone with her thoughts and the whisky. She discovered her hands were shaking. Of course, she thought, he is thinking of himself and his own woman – wife – who left him when he was injured. It would be difficult, perhaps impossible, for anyone as young as he had been when it happened to separate the one thing from the other. Now he was seeing Heinz in the same position. But who knows why his wife had left him? Perhaps she didn't love him. Perhaps she didn't want to ally herself with a cripple. At any rate, she had not allowed herself to be blackmailed either, though doubtless George, having been the sufferer, wouldn't have seen it as blackmail.

She sighed, wondering what would become of them. It was a mess. Poor Heinz was in as bad a mess as any of them, of course, but she had to save some pity for George and for herself. In a sense they were the victims – what had happened to Heinz was, if not his own choice, at least his own fault.

The next time George came in, it was with the food, and Clover was aware that she was drunk. He had cooked macaroni rings with a nice mess of diced chicken and ham with onions and other vegetables all in a kind of sauce. He put down the two plates on the table to one side of the room, and Clover heaved herself over there and sat down.

'I didn't know you could cook,' she said. He smiled tersely.

'All Scotsmen can cook. It's in their blood. Now eat, woman.'

'Ooh, I do love it when you're masterful,' she murmured, reaching for her fork and missing. He looked at her in surprise.

144

'You're drunk,' he said.

'I am under the affluence of incohol,' she said with dignity, 'but then it's your incohol, and so that makes it your fault.'

'I love your logic,' he said. 'Anyway, eat.'

She did. 'It's delicious,' she said, and forked it down ravenously.

'Don't sound surprised — it's an insult. And don't eat so fast, you'll get hiccoughs.'

'Keep telling me things,' she said between mouthfuls. 'It makes me feel secure.'

'You can't feel secure with me,' he said.

'Why the hell not?' she said. 'You don't have to answer that. In any case, I see you can't. The thing is, with all this good Scotch inside me, I can afford to be outrageous and speak the truth, even though I'm perfectly well aware I may regret it tomorrow. And regret it or not, I have to say that I do feel secure with you, especially when you're telling me what to do like a stern parent.'

'Parent be damned,' he muttered, and she thought, oh goody, he doesn't feel paternal towards me. That's a start. 'Look,' he said, 'outrageous or not, if you mean what I think you mean, I still don't see how you could expect me to feel right about taking you away from him, when it's largely my fault he's in the state he's in. And when you consider my past history in fact, if there was nothing else to consider, that alone ought to tell you what's going through my mind.'

She gaped at him, and the fork she had just loaded unloaded itself with a graceful slither back on to the plate.

'Eat your dinner,' he said.

'Listen,' she said, 'everything - every single thing you just said - is wrong. There's so much wrong with it, I don't know which bit to start refuting first. For God's sake, George -'

She emptied her glass again, and George, seeing her reach for it just too late, removed the empty glass when she put it down and said, 'I think you've had enough whisky. You aren't making sense.'

145

'It isn't me,' she said indignantly. 'Apart from anything else, it's as much tiredness as anything. And I still know what I'm saying. I know what you're saying, too, which is more to the point. How can you even begin to talk about *taking me away* from someone, as if I was a teddy-bear or something? You kindly allow me to decide who I belong to, if anyone can belong to anyone else, which I sincerely doubt. You're as bad as him, saying "Clover's mine!" on top of a mountain for anyone to hear. All right, it may be flattering and so on, but only when I tell you when.'

She realised that this hadn't come out quite as coherently as she'd wished, and George was looking at her with an expression of suppressed amusement which, though it was better than his superior gravity, was still not the way he was supposed to be looking. She finished the macaroni dish and felt pleasantly full, and extremely tired.

'I've forgotten what else you said,' she admitted at last.

'You have?'

'But it was wrong, all of it, whatever it was. You shouldn't take advantage of me, you know. It isn't fair. Oh God, George, I'm terribly, terribly tired.'

Even as she said it, she could feel herself slipping away. Through a blur she saw George jump up and rush round the table to her, and felt his arms supporting her.

'You really have had it, haven't you?' she heard him say. 'Poor kid.'

I'm not a kid, she said, but it didn't actually come out. She relaxed against him, and with the minimum of self-help allowed him to draw her out from her seat and gather her up in his arms. She was not as limp as she allowed him to think, but on the other hand, what was the point in struggling against it? She put her arms round his neck and leaned her head against his shoulder.

'Nice,' she murmured. 'Are you taking me to bed George?'

'Hush, you wanton,' he said, gently teasing. 'You come here and drink my booze and then try to compromise me –?'

'Oh no,' she murmured. 'I'd never compromise you.'

146

'Because I'm too nice.'

'Because you're too careful.'

'That makes too much sense for a girl as tired and drunk as you are,' he said. 'Here we are, now. Bed.'

He put her down on the bed, took off her shoes, socks, trousers and jumper, and slid her into bed in her underwear. It was so nice to be looked after that she really couldn't feel anything other than sleepiness. If he gets into bed, she thought, I'll have to make the effort, after he's been so kind. But that was the last thing she did manage to think, and if he got into bed with her later, she was certainly not to know anything about it, so deeply asleep as she was.

TWELVE

THE NEXT thing she knew she was being wakened by George who stood over her, fully dressed, and holding a tumbler of something in which ice clinked. She groaned.

'Haven't you got any quiet ice?'

'You feel terrible,' he informed her.

'Tell me something I don't know. I was having the most horrible dream. I was trying to organise a football match in outer space.'

'Sounds frustrating,' he said.

'It was,' she said. 'I ask you, how can you have a football match where there are no intelligent life forms?'

'Millwall manage it,' he said. 'Here, drink this.'

'In films people always say "Drink this" when you come round,' she said, sitting up. It was orange juice. She drank thirstily. 'God that's good. I don't feel half so bad now.'

He was studying her quizzically, and a new thought came into her mind. She found herself blushing.

'Last night,' she said. 'Did I – did you –?'

'You got drunk,' he said. 'I slept on the sofa.'

She considered the leather Chesterfield as a site of downy repose.

'Oh,' she said. 'It doesn't sound very comfortable.'

'No, but the buttons give you a lovely pattern on your skin. You'd better get up now, or you'll be late for work, and you don't want the Commandant after you, do you?'

She grinned unwillingly. 'Stop it. I can't cope with *déjà entendu* this early in the morning.'

He threw her a silk dressing-gown from behind the door. 'Here you are. You head for the bathroom.'

148

'Oh, you are decent,' she said, swinging her legs out of bed cautiously. It really wasn't too bad after all.

'I should have a bath if I were you, and I'll cook you some breakfast, but you really will have to hurry.'

'Breakfast?' she said doubtfully.

'Breakfast,' he said firmly. 'When you're suffering from mild alcoholic poisoning, which is what a hangover is, you need a hot bath, a good meal and plenty of liquids. Take my word for it – I'm a Scot, we're born hung over.'

She stood up, wrapping the dressing-gown round her. 'This is just the goonie I would have expected you to have,' she said. She stopped and looked up at him. 'When I said you are decent, I meant you are decent. Thank you.'

He looked down at her, and for a moment his eyes were so caressing that she thought he was going to kiss her. But the moment passed and he only gave a little nod and turned away, heading for the kitchen.

Ten minutes later she was dressed and sitting at the table with a plate of the most delicious scrambled eggs she had ever tasted in front of her. She wanted very badly to say I love you, George, but was aware that scrambled eggs were not considered socially enough justification. So she ate while he sat opposite, watching her, elbows on the table and chin in hands in what was for him an unexpectedly youthful attitude.

'I was up early today,' he said at last.

'I would imagine you'd want to be after a night with the buttons.'

'Buttons? Oh, yes. Well, I've made a few phone calls and some arrangements for today. I'm taking a class of advanced skiers up on to the Enzianberg runs, and I'm going to take you with me, too.'

She raised an eyebrow. 'Pulling rank, eh?'

'I want to keep an eye on you,' he said, and then gave an unwilling smile. 'All right, I want to keep you with me.'

'Better. And what's the excuse for public consumption?'

'Large class of advanceds – I need an extra supervisor.'

'Ho yuss,' she said. 'What happens to my class?'

'I've split them up and spread them round. They don't

149

know yet, but I've got Hilary phoning round the hotels with messages, and Val is telling the other lehrers.'

'Let's hope the crew won't mutiny at the Captain keeping his woman aboard,' she said. He looked uncomfortable.

'It isn't that,' he began.

'I know,' she said. 'I'm teasing you. Though we'd better be careful going out – if anyone sees us leaving together they'll never believe you slept on the sofa, not even if you show your scars.'

'They'll already know. I told Val you were here, and of course Rose was with him, so everyone will know by lunchtime.'

'Oh dear.'

'What makes you think I mind? It'll do my reputation good. And now, if you have finished, we'd better get moving. You've still got to go back to the hotel and change into your salopette, don't forget. You can't ski like that.'

'Omigod, yes, I had forgotten.'

'I'll drive you down there, and wait for you outside. You can have precisely five minutes to change, no longer. We've still got to go to the office and make sure everything's sorted out, though I'm sure Hilary will have performed as efficiently as usual. Still, I have to check.'

When they reached the school office, the first person they saw was Rose, standing outside with her class. When Clover got out of George's car she came over to her.

'You,' she said, giving Clover a roguish jab with the elbow. Clover lifted her hands innocently.

'He slept on the sofa.' Rose cocked a knowing eye at her.

'You must take me for an idiot.'

'That sounds like a fair exchange.'

'And what have you done with my car?'

Clover stared blankly, and then laughed. 'I'd forgotten entirely about it until this moment,' she said. 'Oh, don't worry, it's outside the apartment house. You could have

150

collected it this morning if I'd thought about it.'
'Thanks a bunch. Listen, Clovella, I'm so glad about you and George.'
'Wait a bit, there isn't anything to be glad about yet; nothing's happened, you know.'
'But it will, won't it?'
'God, I hope so,' she said. 'I really hope so.' She looked more closely at her friend, and smiled. 'You're looking very well on whatever's happening to you. And *I'm* so glad about *that*.'
Rose smiled. She looked, already, gentler, rounder, less angular, less untidy, less eccentric.
'He's lovely,' she said. 'I think I'm in love for the first time in my life.'
'Well, he seems to be making you conventional,' Clover said.
'Better than making you conventual, like your George,' Rose replied with spirit. 'Still, there's all day today.'
'And tonight,' Clover said. 'I'm not going to the hospital – which reminds me, I meant to ask Ernst if he'd do a visit.'
'I'm sure he will,' Rose said. 'I'll ask him if you like – we've both got classes on the nursery slopes today.'
'Thanks,' Clover said. Rose looked curiously at her.
'Heinz let you off the leash, then?'
'Neither off the leash nor off the hook. I've mutinied. Even if I'd wanted to go, I don't think I ought to.'
'Oh. Like that,' Rose said. 'I wondered about that, before it happened even. You'll remember I warned you.'
'Yes,' Clover said. 'But I don't see really what I could have done.'
'Me neither. There's your master calling. Good luck, kid.'
'With the class you mean?' Clover said innocently. Rose grinned.
'They didn't tell me you were giving lessons in it now.'
'Garn!' Clover said. 'I'm a good girl, I am.'
The atmosphere between her and George that day was one she couldn't quite define. It was easy and friendly,

almost intimate, but yet not the kind of air that existed between acknowledged lovers. Though there was no coldness, not even the shadow of it, in the way he was with her, she still got the feeling that he was holding back something. There was still a reserve, too deep under the surface for her to be able to tap; she wondered if he was still troubled about her relationship with Heinz, or still feeling in some way responsible for the accident.

They did the long lift journey up to the top of the Enzianberg, and gathered the class round them. Clover stood a pace to the rear, watching him as he answered questions, checked equipment, laughed at jokes, and waited for them to settle down and give them his attention so that he could tell them what to do. It was fascinating. There was about him an air of quiet authority which gave confidence; he ought perhaps to have been a teacher or a minister or a leader of men. Clover thought, too, that he ought to have children of his own, lots of them. He would make a terrific father.

Taking a class as advanced as this one she saw was very different from the beginners' classes she had been instructing. It was much more like the kind of teaching she had been giving at the rink, each pupil being dealt with individually by the lehrer in turn. They all practised the thing they felt they needed most and asked George for advice and criticism, and Clover saw how much effort went into keeping track of each of them as well as maintaining overall discipline. She soon spotted George's trouble-spot, given that there was one Piet to each class, on average. It was a tall, heavily built young man wearing a racing-suit who, though not a bad skier, seemed out to impress everyone and in the process got in everyone's way.

During a pause Clover asked George quietly what he did about someone like that, and he shrugged.

'Barry?' he said. 'It's difficult. You can't really tell him off, even quietly, because it just antagonises him. All you can do with people like that is to try and steer them into practising manoeuvres they can manage, and stand by to bail them out – and anyone they take with them.'

During the afternoon clouds began to gather in the sky and after a while it began to snow lightly. Clover noticed George casting an eye towards the sky now and then and concluded he was worried about the weather, and sure enough at about half past three he skied over to her and said, 'I think the clouds are closing in, and we'd better get them down. We're higher here than on Rosenberg. Can you help me round them up and head for the lifts?'

'Okay,' Clover said, and poled off towards the nearest group of girls. They were standing chattering and had already, by the look of them, given up on ski-ing for the afternoon.

'It looks as though it's going to come on heavily,' one of them said. 'I'm not sorry to be packing up.'

A quarter of an hour later Clover joined George by the ski-lift station at the bottom of the highest run, and the snow was crusting their heads and shoulders quite thickly.

'We'd better go down too, hadn't we?' she asked, looking forward to a hot bath and a mug of *gluhwein* herself. 'Are we all present and correct?'

He gave a grim little smile. 'Not quite. Barry hasn't come down yet.'

'Where is he?'

'He saw me calling everyone in and straight away headed for the drag again. Wanted to come down the run one last time, I suppose.'

Clover turned round and stared through the snow up the mountain. 'I can't see him,' she said. George turned sharply and peered forward.

'Damn and blast. He must have gone off the piste. What a pain in the neck these youngsters are.' He looked around, watching another two girls hitching themselves on to a lift, and then said, 'Well, we can't leave him up there. This is getting worse. I'd better go up and look for him.'

'Not alone,' Clover said. 'I'm coming with you. Is everyone else accounted for?'

'All of mine. I don't know if there are any other non-class skiers around, but they aren't my responsibility. Come on, then, let's get the drag. And what ever you do, keep with me – don't get separated.'

'As if I would,' Clover said. 'I was only afraid you would refuse to let me come with you.'

'I'm glad you offered. I wouldn't like to search alone for a lone skier, just in case.'

They took the drag up through increasingly heavy snow to the top of the run, and with George leading they began to ski in wide shallow loops across the breadth of the first slope. It was no use trying to find Barry's tracks – there were too many of them, and all were quickly being obliterated by the snow falling – but they called and listened alternately, hoping Barry was not too far off the piste to hear them. Then George called her over to the edge of the trail.

'It looks as though this is where he left the piste,' he said. 'These are the only marks I've found that go off it. He was heading in that direction.'

Clover looked, and then squinted ahead, shaking her head.

'Can't see anything. Of course, I don't know this mountain very well. I don't know where he'd be heading.'

'I don't suppose he did either,' George said. 'Unless he was hoping to ski round the shoulder to the red run. Still, we'll go a little way, see if we can find any more tracks.'

They started off, and only seconds later all visibility was suddenly shut off as if with a switch, and they were in the middle of a white-out. Even Clover, who knew what had happened, was startled and frightened. She snow-ploughed to a halt, caught her breath, and then shouted. There was no reply to her first call, and she had to fight down the panic for a few seconds before she could call again.

'George! George!'

'All right. I hear you. Start counting, and I'll come to you.'

His voice sounded incredibly small and distant, but she began to count aloud, steadily, and he reached her before ten, coming out of the wall of cloud and falling snow like a ghost. Clover grabbed his hand unashamedly.

'Oh, that was horrible. Like going deaf in your eyes,'

she said.

'I know what you mean,' he said. 'Beastly stuff, isn't it? Well, we'll never find him now.'

'Don't worry, he's probably down already. People like that never come to any harm, worst luck. They lead charmed existences. It's other people who suffer for their misdeeds.'

'Like us, you mean?' George said. 'You realise I now have no idea where we are. I've completely lost my sense of direction.'

'Don't joke on serious subjects,' Clover said. He looked gravely down into her snow-dusted face.

'I'm not joking, I'm afraid. I don't know which way I'm facing any more, and this part of the mountain being flat, I don't even know which way is downhill.'

'Oh,' said Clover in a small voice. She held on tighter to his hand, and then said, more cheerfully, 'But if we go on, one way or the other, we're bound either to start going uphill or downhill, aren't we? And then we'll know, and we can point ourselves downhill until we get out of the cloud.'

'Clever girl,' he said. 'Except that it's now snowing so hard I don't think getting out of the cloud will help. We can't ski down in this. I think we had better try going along the flat. One way we should eventually come to the cables, and the other way – well I happen to know there's an avalanche hut not far from where I think we were when the white-out happened. We can't just stand still, anyway. The essential thing is not to get separated.'

He had a piece of cord in his bum-bag, which he tied on to his belt, and gave the end into Clover's hand, and then began to langlauf forward through the thick settled snow. From time to time they stopped and listened, hoping to hear the sound of the cables running, and called, in case anyone else was near, but they heard nothing. Clover had not been worried at first, but as the snowfall got thicker and heavier she began to be a little afraid. It was coming down so thickly that she had continually to clear her goggles, and tilting her head downwards she could barely

155

see her own skis. After a while, they found themselves moving faster, and realised they were heading down hill, though Clover had no idea where they were or which way they were facing, she hadn't even any idea of how long they had been moving. Time in that sightless white world didn't have any reference any more than direction did.

George was moving more slowly and cautiously, prodding ahead of him with his poles, and then he stopped again and turned to her, beckoning her alongside him.

'I'm afraid of going over the edge if we go on,' he said. 'I don't know if we were going towards the cables or away from them, but if it was away, we must be near the shoulder by now, and there's a steep drop beyond it.'

'What shall we do, then?' she asked. 'Perhaps we could build some sort of shelter for ourselves with the snow, like an igloo.'

'Wrong sort of snow,' he said, with a brief smile. 'No we'd – wait! What's that, over there? Do you see something dark?'

Clover stared in the direction he pointed, but could not make out anything.

'I don't think so. I don't see anything but snow.' They both stared, and then at the same moment cried out, as a momentary eddy in the fall revealed the vaguest dark shadow up ahead. 'Yes, there!'

'Come on,' George said, staring forward again. They shuffled onwards, and again time seemed to stop, and Clover was sure they had missed whatever object they had sighted. Then, abruptly, the dark shape was there again, very near; two more steps, and it became the wooden side of the avalanche hut.

'Thank God,' George said, and the relief in his voice showed Clover how much anxiety he had been concealing for her sake.

'You know where you are now, then?' Clover said. 'You can make a bearing to get us down?'

He shook his head. 'It'll be getting dark soon,' he said. 'We'll have to shelter here, at least until the snow stops. We'd get hopelessly lost, in a storm like this, in the dark, if

156

we tried to go down. Come on, let's get inside. These places aren't bad, you know. We'll be warm.'

They struggled round the side of the hut until they found the door, and George lifted the great wooden latch, and they went in, shutting out the storm behind them and finding themselves in sudden stillness and darkness, for as well as the problem of the fading light, the windows were caked with snow. George bent down to take off his skis, and then said, 'There'll be a lamp somewhere. Get your skis off, and then we can get a fire going. We'll be all right here. They stock them up with firewood and things.'

It was a bare little hut, made of wood like a pioneer's cabin, with a stone fireplace and a couple of wooden benches. Cupboards in the walls revealed some blankets, a couple of hurricane lamps, and some dry stores. There were logs piled in the fireplace, and another door opened into a tiny store-room beyond which there was a can of paraffin and some more firewood. George lit both the lamps and hung them up, and then set about lighting the fire, for which Clover was grateful, for she was beginning to shiver.

'These places used to be well stocked a few years ago, with food and stuff in case anyone got trapped in foul weather or by avalanches, but people kept stealing things, and now they're left with the bare minimum.'

'Couldn't the things have been left locked up?' Clover said. George raised an eyebrow.

'Provided only people with a key got lost,' he said. She shook her head.

'Silly of me. I was just thinking how terrible that people in trouble should suffer because of other people's dishonesty.'

'I'm afraid that's the way of the world nowadays. There now, that's caught. That'll burn up nicely in a minute. Now, shall we see what stores there are?'

There were quite a number of tins, but they all turned out to be empty, except for a tin of ships biscuits and two tins of condensed soup.

'Pity,' George said. 'I hoped there might be some tea or

coffee. Well, we can boil up some snow and drink hot water – that'll warm us up. And I've got some chocolate in by bum-bag. We'd better leave the soup for now.'

Clover almost asked why, and then thought that he probably meant in case they were trapped there for days, in which case she didn't want to know. George opened the door briefly on the dark and snowy world to scoop some snow into a saucepan, and then put it on the trivet to boil, and they pulled the benches up near the fire, which was blazing up nicely now.

When the water was hot, George poured it into two plastic mugs, and gave one to Clover. It seemed strange to be drinking hot water with nothing in it, but he was quite right – it did very quickly warm her up, and drunk in between bites at a slab of chocolate George gave her it was not unpleasant. The bench was uncomfortable to sit on, though, and she soon abandoned that for a seat on the floor, on one of the blankets, and after a while George, without a word, slid down beside her, and they remained in companionable silence, staring at the flickering flames.

'Well,' she said at last, 'we seem to be stuck here for the moment. Should we play games or sing or something, to keep our spirits up?'

George smiled. 'You are quaint,' he said. 'Why should you think my spirits need keeping up?'

'Don't they?'

'Of course not. Here I am, trapped alone up a mountain with a beautiful woman. My only fear is that the snow will stop too soon.'

'Oh. Well, we could always not bother to look,' she said.

'But they'll be worried about us down below. And if the snow stops, they may even come looking for us.'

'Nasty spoil-sports,' she smiled. 'In that case, we'd better make the most of it while we can. I've got some whisky in my bum-bag.'

'Why didn't you say so before?' he demanded indignantly.

'Because all the books say you mustn't take alcohol if

158

you're trapped in the snow.'

'True, but we're inside now, safe, warm and dry. Hoik it out, woman, and let's have a wee drop to keep our spirits up.'

Grinning, Clover reached for her bum-bag and delved in amongst the bandages and sticking-plasters and silverwax and pen-knife and length of nylon cord for the little plastic bottle she had filled with whisky from a half-bottle she kept in her room, and handed it over to George. He unscrewed it and handed it back politely to her saying, 'Ladies first.'

'Thanks.' She took a swig and passed it back.

'Cheers.' He drank. 'Ah, that's the stuff. Now we have all we need to sit out a couple of hours. Are you all right there on that blanket? There's another one here, if the floor's too hard.'

'No, I'm all right. How's the snow getting on?'

He went to the window for a look.

'Nicely. I don't think we can go for a while yet. It seems to have settled in for the present.'

'How long can it keep snowing like that?'

'Anything from an hour to four hours,' he said coming back to the fire and looking down at her. 'Would you say that was long enough?'

'She patted the blanket beside her.

'Sit down, and I'll tell you,' she said.

THIRTEEN

SHE LOOKED up, and their eyes met with that peculiar meeting which is never arrived at by effort. George turned a little paler, and Clover suddenly felt the heat of the fire as if she was too near it.

'Don't,' he said quietly. 'It's dangerous.'

She shook her head dumbly and indicated again the place on the blanket beside her. He sighed and sat down unwillingly, as if his limbs were pulling him down against his will.

'I've tried to avoid this,' he said, and his voice was small as if coming from a long way away.

'Why?'

'Because –' he looked uncomfortable. 'Because perhaps I'm too old fashioned. I can't do it lightly. It will seem absurd to you –'

'No.'

'But it isn't a casual thing with me. Don't make me.' He had been looking away, anywhere but at her, and now he turned his face to her to appeal and lost himself again. 'You're trembling.'

She was. He stared for a moment longer, and then put his arms round her as one might to a child, drawing her against him. Perhaps he really thought she was cold or distressed; perhaps he managed to convince himself for a moment that she was; but then her hands came up blindly to his shoulders, his breath went out of him in a little rush, and their faces nuzzled round for each other like newborn pups, searching, finding, frantic mouth to mouth.

Sitting awkwardly, holding on to each other to keep

160

their balance, they kissed in the firelight in a small hut at the heart of a storm which was their protection. After a while George drew breath, and gently eased her back on to the blanket to lie beside her, only because it was more comfortable. He went on kissing her as if he would never stop. In love as she was, the watchdog in her brain told her distantly that what happened here would be decisive. She felt him growing more calm; if he stepped back from her again, she might never be able to break down the barrier he had put up around himself.

If she did nothing, he would withdraw. If she did the wrong thing, he would withdraw. Perhaps he felt her tension, for he stopped kissing her, leaned up on his elbow and looked down into her face with an expression she had seen before: watchful, enquiring. The firelight ran like water over his face, fingers drawing it out of the darkness, creating and recreating the contours and features. His hair was ruffled, his lips parted. What to do or say? And it was instinct that saved her, a sudden rush of emotion that flooded her brain and washed away all considerations of now or the future.

'I love you,' she whispered, and her voice sounded faint as if with pain. He stared, and then almost in terror she saw him breaking. He closed his eyes, and put his mouth to hers, and held her so tightly she could not breathe.

'Oh, my darling,' he whispered.

Kissing again; this time not in desperation, but that wild seeking, two bodies no longer able to bear their separateness, trying to be each other. Hands sought out flesh, only not to be kept apart by clothing; touching and stroking in a wonder that anything could be so beautiful and so beloved; eyes, mouth and hands following each other in exploration, in astonished joy of discovery. Only then desire came, an extra guest who had been waiting a long time at the door, not knowing if there was room for him.

They did not know each other's bodies, but there was no difficulty, no clumsiness to cool them. They undressed, sometimes themselves and sometimes each other, and naked in the firelight took time again to look and touch in

161

wonder. Then they stretched their bodies against each other and he slid into her as easily as a creature moving in its own, known element.

'Oh, God,' Clover cried out softly. The sensation was so terrifyingly exotic that she thought she must die under it from the bewilderment of her senses, it was both known and strange, the familiar touch of his body and the alien penetration, the possession of her body that was a violation. He moved, and filled her with an unbearable pleasure. She held on to him as if he might save her, pressing her face to him in supplication as if it was not he who was moving inside her, causing this strange disintegration.

Possessed, and lost; she began to cry out, and the invasion grew, reaching forward into her body through the channels of feeling. His mouth came round for hers, and their tongues arched together, and she felt through his mouth the quality of his suffering, as great as hers, but different. She began to move helplessly, neither with nor against the unendurable pleasure, but through it as if it was where she was. She spoke and heard him speak too, and she found then what she was; she was him. To let another person inside your body is a violation of that animal integrity that all creatures have and without which they die, as wild creatures die in captivity only because they have been touched and so violated. He was in her, inside her, and at the point when it was no longer to be borne all the barriers dissolved, melted away, and he was her, their magic circles broken, each self yielded, dispersed, diffused. He came in her, crying out, and the possession was perfect, one body between two, and that body not flesh but pure sensation.

They took a long time to come back, drifting slowly down into the outposts of their bodies, becoming aware of their labouring lungs and pounding hearts. She moved and felt the weight of him on her, the moistness of his skin against her, the hard dry smoothness of his broad back under her hands, the soft prickle of his hair against her cheek, the undemanding shape of his penis inside her. His

162

breathing was stabilising, his muscles relaxing. She smelled the animal scent of him, and knew that she would never forget it, that from now on it would be the scent that called her as an animal finds its way home. She was filled with a vast tenderness, a sense of vulnerability which is another thing that we call love. She moved, stroking him, because she was suddenly lonely, wanted him back from wherever his relaxation had taken him.

George felt the demand and recognised it. He turned his face on her shoulder and kissed her cheek, opening his eyes while moving a hand to stroke her hair.

'Did you mean it?' he asked after a while.

She didn't have to ask what he meant.

'Yes,' she said. 'Couldn't you tell?'

'It's hard to know if a thing is real or if it's only how you imagine it would be.'

'I've never felt like this with anyone else,' she said. He knew how vulnerable she was making herself so that he should not be afraid. How easy it would be to draw back, how tempting it was to run away. He lifted himself a little to look down at her and their skins squeaked apart with their mixed sweat. They were as close as two human beings can be. He was still inside her. She looked up at him without apprehension. He felt suddenly weak, a warmth welling inside him as if the boulder had been rolled away from a deep spring so that it came surging up, gushing into the light. What had happened here was for ever. What ever happened now, he would never feel the same about anything again.

'I love you,' he said. Such inadequate words; but a code, all the same, for all the sensation, the weakness, the warmth, the sense of having been away on a long journey and of having come home, the tired pleasurable jangling of nerve-ends, the sweet mingled smell of sweat and sex, the feasting of the eyes on what was newly and significantly beautiful, the sensation of not being alone. 'I love you.' There was a luxury in saying it. He saw the skin under her eyes draw up in the loving shadow of a smile.

'Yes,' she said. 'And I love you. Oh, George – I'm so glad!'

163

He slid over on to the blanket and drew her against him, settling her in the hollow of his arms, and she rested her head on his shoulder and he leaned his cheek against the top of her head. She sighed and he felt her relax deeply. She felt such repose there. She leaned against him confidingly, trusting that the strength of his body would be gentle to her nakedness.

The logs collapsed together in a mass of glowing jewels, and Clover woke from a doze and shivered violently. George jerked awake too, and they both sat up and with one accord reached for their clothes.

'We weren't asleep very long,' Clover reassured herself aloud. George, having pulled on his ski trousers and jumper got up and went to the door and opened it carefully.

'It's stopped snowing,' he said. She joined him and looked out. The night was as clear and black as well-water and utterly still under the blue pin-pricks of stars, and the heaped snow glittered away on every side, fantastic and inviting, like a feather bed with a crushed-diamond coverlet. It was beautiful, but its beauty was so vast and untouchable that it was exhausting to Clover, and she longed for something human-sized and cosy.

'Can we go down?' she asked. George looked about, scenting the air like a hound.

'I think there's enough light,' he said. 'We've only to get to the cables, and then we'll be able to see the lights of the village below.' He glanced at her with sudden amusement. 'You want to go down? You don't want to stay for ever on top of a mountain with me?'

'No, Endymion,' she said. 'I want an enormous meal and a hot bath, and then I want to get into your lovely big comfortable bed with you and make love and sleep.'

'You brazen woman,' he said, smiling. 'You're trying to corrupt me. Come on, then, let's get our skis on. I must say the evening you've just sketched out for us exactly corresponds to the one I had in mind.'

'All of it?'

'All of it,' he said firmly.

'Oh good.'

In companionable silence they went back in, finished dressing, folded up the blankets, spoored the fire, tidied everything away, and then put on their skis and went out into the cold, clear night. It was hard going at first, the snow being bottomless, and like Wenceslas's boy, Clover skied in George's tracks where the snow lay dinted. She was enormously, vibrantly happy as well as incredibly tired. Everything was going to be all right now; they only had to get this difficult bit of the journey over with, and then a long straightforward downhill run to the village, and comfort. He had said he loved her; it would be all right. It is so strange, she thought as she laboured along, that in this situation the words are so much more important than the actions. A man can lie with you, and do every loving thing one person can do to another, but unless he says the words, none of it counts.

She bumped into the back of George's skis and exclaimed crossly.

'What's the matter?' she asked. He had stopped and was staring away to the left.

'What's that?' he said after a moment. She looked.

'What's what?'

'That heap of snow. Over there.'

'It's a heap of snow,' she said after due consideration. 'Let's go on.'

But he didn't move. 'No,' he said. 'I think I'll just go and have a look.'

Clover grew uneasy. 'Don't,' she said. 'Let's go on. I want to get home. I want a bath.'

But he turned out of the line and began to pole himself towards the object, if object it was, and sighing crossly Clover heaved herself after him. When she floundered up to him, he was crouched, digging at the snow with his hands. It wasn't really much of a heap of snow, just a slight divergence in the surface line, and waiting for him, yawning, she wondered what had attracted him to it in the

165

first place.

Then he stiffened, and gave a muttered exclamation, and dug and brushed harder at the snow. Clover stared, her eyes getting bigger. Inside the heap of snow was Barry, huddled up, dead. She had completely forgotten about him.

From the lift-station they telephoned down, and as soon as the cables whined into action George sent Clover on down the mountain. She wanted to stay with him, but he would not let her. He gave her the key to his apartment, and said, 'There's food there. Have your hot bath and your meal, and get into bed. Get some rest. You've had a very hard day of it, and I don't want you getting ill.'

'What about you?' Clover asked, feeling colder inside than out.

'I'll be busy for a long time yet. I'll have to wait and show them where the body is, and then there'll be umpteen things to do – see the police, get a doctor to give a certificate, fill in a report, get on to his people. It'll take hours.'

'You need something to eat and some rest too,' she pointed out angrily. 'You have had a hard day too. Let someone else do it.'

'It's my responsibility,' he said. She looked up into his face and saw how remote he was from her. She was now simply a nuisance, another thing he had to deal with. Her anger dissolved, and, not to be a burden, she nodded and turned away to the lift, feeling as if a lump of ice was lodged in the bottom of her belly. All the warmth and intimacy of their lovemaking was gone, and they were strangers again, two extremely separate people. Wrapped in that loneliness, she went down the mountain and to George's apartment, to eat, bathe, and get wearily into bed. She felt no pity or sorrow for Barry – all her thoughts were with the tired man waiting alone at the top of the mountain to bring a corpse home.

166

When she woke, it was light and she was alone in bed. The clock on the bedside table had stopped, presumably because it hadn't been wound, and she groped for her watch and discovered it was ten past nine. She sat up, and at that moment heard the sound of the kitchen door opening, shortly preceding the smell of coffee and the appearance of George in the doorway with a tray. It must have been some sound he made that wakened her. He looked grey and tired and he came round to the empty side of the bed and put the tray down without a smile or greeting.

'Coffee,' he said, as if it was all the information she needed. He poured out two cups and gave her one, and she saw by the way he lifted his cup to his mouth that it was all he saw between himself and collapse. The coffee was very strong and very hot and she sipped it gratefully.

'Where did you sleep?' she asked at length.

'I haven't yet,' he said. 'There's been too much to do. You slept well?'

'Like a log. I was exhausted.'

'It's late. You'd better get a move on or you'll keep your class waiting. Can you get your bathroom bits done now, so that I can have a bath?'

'Okay,' she said, subdued. It was as if nothing had happened between them. Perhaps he was regretting it. Worse, perhaps he had forgotten it. Worst, perhaps she had imagined it. She got carefully out of bed, avoiding looking at him.

'I'll be five minutes, that's all,' she said carefully. He grunted but did not answer, sipping at his coffee. She went into the bathroom and had a quick wash and then turned on the bath for him, searching around for something to put in it and finding some Radox. The steam at once smelt herbal and soothing. When it was full she tested for temperature and called out to him, 'Bath's ready.' She waited until she heard him come out of the bedroom, and then added, 'While you bath I'll cook some breakfast,' and went into the kitchen, closing the door to leave him his privacy. The kitchen was immaculate and as spare and

167

convenient as a ship's galley. There was the remains of a ham joint in the fridge, and she cut slices, pink and flaky, from near the bone, and poached some eggs, and sliced a couple of tomatoes. She cut bread and buttered it, and found a pot of honey, and when she heard him come out of the bathroom she took everything through to the sitting room and laid it out on the table. He came to her call, dressed in his silk gown.

'Did you put on more coffee?' he asked.

'No,' she said. 'The percolator was in the bedroom. I forgot.'

He went through and got it and took it to the kitchen and returned a moment later to sit down without a word and consume the food she had put out. Despite his tiredness he seemed very hungry, and she guessed he hadn't eaten last night either. He did not speak until she had finished eating, and then he said, 'You'd better get dressed. It's a quarter to ten.'

She got up and went to the bedroom to dress, tears prickling her eyes. He was so cold he seemed hostile, as if he wanted nothing to do with her. He must be regretting what had happened. Perhaps, in his absurd way, manlike, he was blaming himself for Barry's death now, along with Heinz's injury. Well, she wouldn't trouble him. She would go to her class, and afterwards she would go back to the Hot Max and keep out of his way. If he hated what had happened, she would not remind him.

She went back through the sitting room, and he was sitting at the table, his head in his hands, looking defeated. Her petulance left her, and she felt pity for him.

'You should go to bed now,' she said gently. He didn't look up.

'Can't,' he said. 'I've got a class. Paying customers.'

She waited, but he didn't say any more, so she left him, and he didn't even notice her going.

She met Rose at lunchtime at the lodge, and to that audience of flattering attention she recounted the whole story of the night before.

168

'My God, things really happen to you, don't they?' Rose said. 'In all the years I've been doing this, nothing even remotely exciting has happened to me, and you come here for the first time, and prance about like the hero of a boy's adventure comic. There's no justice.'

'I don't suppose Barry thinks there is either,' Clover said. Rose looked indignant.

'He caused enough trouble. He could have got you two killed. I'm sorry, of course, that it came to that, but there's some kinds of stupidity I've no sympathy with.'

'I've no sympathy with my own,' Clover said. 'I should never have told him I loved him. It's frightened him off. Men are such strange creatures, you never know what to do for the best.'

'Oh, come on, Clovesy, don't be so glum. I'm sure it isn't that. He was just tired, I expect. It's been tough for him. You know he takes everything very seriously.'

'But he was completely indifferent to me this morning. I didn't expect him to be sweeping me off my feet, but he barely glanced at me, and he didn't even say goodbye when I left, or see you later, or anything to show he ever wanted to see me again.'

'Of course he wants to see you again. Kid, he wouldn't have screwed you if he didn't feel something for you, now would he?'

Clover made a face. 'God, it sounds so awful. I don't know – people do it all the time, don't they? Why should I expect him to be any different?'

Rose grinned. 'If that's your only worry, don't worry. George is different all right. He's the differentest person I ever saw.'

'I think he's regretting it, and he was feeling embarrassed this morning. The sight of me upset him. Well, I won't make it worse. I'll keep out of his way.'

Rose sighed and shook her head. 'You do give Cupid a hard time, you older people. You should take a tip from us youngsters – impale yourself on the arrow, and get it over with.'

At the end of the day Clover sought out Rose and went

down the mountain with her. They walked back to the hotel, talking eagerly, Clover neither looking to left nor right so that no one should be able to point a finger afterwards. Clover took her bath, lingered over changing in case her room telephone should ring, and then went down to the restaurant and sat alone at the bar, lingering over a Scotch until the other lehrers came in for dinner. But *he* didn't appear, and no message came, and she chided herself for having even despite herself expected one.

The other lehrers wanted to hear the story of Barry, so she had to tell it all over again, and they treated her with sympathetic respect and afterwards allowed her her silence and preoccupation, chattering amongst themselves and not expecting her to join in. Rose wasn't there, and Clover assumed that she was dining with Val again, as she often had these past few days. The waiter removed Clover's untouched soup bowl and replaced it with a plate of veal. She picked at it, and then felt tears prickling her eyes. Hastily she excused herself and slid out from the table and bolted for the loo.

When she had recovered she went back to the bar, unable to face the dinner table. Ernst came over to her and slipped an arm round her shoulders and asked her quite gently if she was all right.

'Yes, thank you,' she said. 'I just want to be on my own.'

'All right,' he said with unexpected delicacy. 'Would you like me to visit Heinz for you again?'

'Oh, yes please,' she said, really grateful. She had been forgetting the old trouble in the heat of the new.

He went back to the table, leaving her alone. She saw the ice-cream being taken across, and was watching the waiters without seeing them when a hand descended on her shoulder and she turned so quickly she almost fell off the stool. It was George, looking more tired than any man she had ever seen, and cross into the bargain.

'What are you doing here?' he demanded irritably. She looked around her in surprise.

'I didn't want any dinner,' she said. 'I thought I'd have

a drink instead.'

Incomprehension spread across his face. He tried again. 'I expected you to be at home. I had to go to the office, and when I got back, you weren't there.'

He meant his home, she realised, with hope struggling back to life.

'At your flat?'

'Of course. I've been looking everywhere for you. Damn it, I was worried. What the hell are you doing here?'

'I didn't know you wanted me,' she said. 'This morning – you didn't say anything. You were so – distant, I thought you were sorry about what had happened and didn't want anything to do with me.'

'Oh God,' he said wearily. 'I'm sorry. But you must be a fool, to think I was sorry about it. I told you – I told you I loved you. Didn't you believe me? I was tired this morning, and depressed. I thought you would understand.'

'I'm sorry,' Clover said, and the tears she had held off slipped past her guard. 'I should have been more sympathetic.'

'Oh, Clover,' he said, reaching out a hand to wipe the tears off her face. 'Poor kid, you must have been suffering all day. I suppose I loved you so much I assumed I didn't need to try. Being with you was so like being alone I didn't feel the need to be polite or explain anything.'

'I'm glad that's what it was. Please go on feeling like that. But, darling George, you must be dead on your feet. You haven't slept.'

He smiled shakily. 'I could do with a nap,' he admitted. 'My car's outside – will you drive me home?'

'Willingly.'

'And stay with me when we get there, of course,' he added. 'I don't want any more misunderstandings.'

'If I can get into bed with you,' she said. 'Just for the company, of course.'

'I don't think I'll be able to resist you. You'd better prepare yourself for more than just company.'

Outside he stopped and turned to her, and put his hands on her shoulders.

'Clover, whatever else you doubt in this world, don't doubt I love you. I told you that I wouldn't do it lightly. I meant it. I love you more than I can possibly tell you. I don't suppose you would marry me, would you?'

Clover smiled happily. 'Try to stop me,' she said.

'Even though I've no future?'

'You have got a future,' she said indignantly. 'What about that hotel we're going to run together in Aviemore? We'll have to start saving up for that.'

His face lit up. 'Would you really like to do that with me? I've got quite a bit of money put aside already, but there never seemed any point in doing anything with it, as long as I was alone.'

'I think it'll be wonderful,' she said. 'We'll be working for ourselves, and our own masters. Shall we really do it?'

He took her hand and tucked it under his arm and walked towards the car.

'I can see it all now,' he said. He was looking straight ahead, but she could see he wasn't seeing Spitalgasse and the Hot Max annexe, and despite his tiredness he looked suddenly younger, gentler, less burdened with irksome responsibility. She loved him so much just then it made her feel quite sick, and weak at the knees. All she wanted was to get to bed. She tugged at his arm, hurrying him, and he came back to the present abruptly, and turned to her with shining eyes.

'My God,' he said, 'think of it! Won't it be marvellous to go home again!'